HE LOVES ME...

Kathey Gray

♡ Kgray

Cover Photo by: Belinda Strange

Cover Model: Stephen Recco

Published by Kathey Gray with Amazon
KDP

He Loves Me... : a novel / by Kathey Gray

"Love, in short is the most dangerous emotion human can experience."
- Virginia C. Andrews

CHAPTER ONE
Maid Of Honor

"Violet, there's someone at the front asking for you."
I hear a voice say.

I peek my head around the dusty book aisle.
"Okay, thanks Jeanette," I say.

She nods at me and hobbles off with her cane. I
feel bad that she had to come all the way over here to
find me and tell me. But I guess it's not customary to
yell across libraries. Jeanette is in her late sixties,
she's been working here for years, she used to work
for my mother before...well, never mind. Anyway,
after a few knee surgeries her knee has seen better
days, hence the cane. I push my black framed glasses
up on my nose and climb over a pile of books on the
floor. I'd been up early sorting through them all day,
preparing for the book sale and stayed up late the
night before. I usually wore contacts but my eyes
were burning too badly to put them in today.

I walk towards the front and see my friend Ava, waving frantically. A smile breaks across my face. Ava has always been the more adventurous one of us two, but we've been friends for years. I've always been secretly a little jealous of her bravery and sense of self. She knows exactly who she is, what she wants and what she doesn't want. I walk towards her, looking up at her slightly, she's easily four inches taller than me.

"I've been trying to get a hold of you!" she scolds me, her thick black mane, swishing behind her as she does.

"Oh, sorry," I smirk. "My phone's been on vibrate." I reach into my pocket for my phone and come up empty. "Actually, where *is* my phone?"

She puts her hands on her hips and raises her brows at me. I grin, sheepishly. "Sorry, I must've lost it in the pile of books. Anyway, what's up?"

A huge smile spreads across her face and her green eyes light up as she holds up her left hand. *"This!"*

My mouth drops as my eyes zero in on her ring finger, a sparkly diamond twinkles on it. "No way, Michael popped the question?"

She tries her best to hold in her squeal. "Yes!"

"Let me see," I breathe. She holds her hand out to me and I inspect the ring, her hand trembles slightly. "You're shaking!" I accuse. "When did this happen?"

"Just now!" she admits.

"Oh my gosh! Well, I'm so honored that you came to tell me! Do your parents know?"

"Yeah, Michael asked them permission," she tilts her head, giggling.

"Wow, how awesome. I'm so happy for you!" We hug and I think that's all the news she has for me until..

"Actually, I have a really important question for *you*..." she says with her eyes wide, smiling conspiratorially.

"Yes?" I smile back, mirroring her expression.

She takes a deep breath. "Will you be my maid of honor?"

I pause for a moment, surprised before answering. "Of course!"

We have a stupid girly moment of jumping up and down, holding hands, until we get some looks from some of the people in the library. We gather our composure. "So when's the wedding?" I ask, wondering when I need to ask off.

"That's the best part, it's in two weeks!" she gushes.

CHAPTER TWO
San Diego

People grieve differently, for me it was to fill the empty hole in my heart with work. Most people thought I was crazy, my father included. He told me to go have fun, live my life. I told him that I *was* living my life. We both knew that was a lie, I was afraid to *really* live. I was afraid to move on.

So when most of my friends moved off to college, I stayed behind. I took over my mom's library, I attended college close to home. I worked on auto pilot, never daring to venture outside of my comfortable safe haven. It wasn't until Ava came bounding in, with all her beauty and vivaciousness, that I felt something again... *excitement*. I can't believe how fast two weeks goes by. I had already performed all of my other "maid of honor" duties, now all that was left was the bachelorette party and the actual wedding. I was in my room packing when my dad walked in.

"You just about packed?" he stood behind me, scratching his beard. I pretty much got my looks from my old man, dark hair and tan skin. My mom was a blonde, but I had the same color blue eyes that she did.

I nodded. "Are you sure you don't want to come?" I eyed him, worried.

"I'm sure honey, besides, someone's got to watch over the library while you're gone," he smiles, affectionately.

I sigh. "Yeah, you're right."

"Quit looking so glum!" my dad laughed. "You're going to *California!* You're supposed to have *fun!*"

"I will dad." I try to convince him *and* myself. Fun...*what was that again?* When was the last time I had *fun?*

"Okay, I'll be waiting in the car when you're ready," he turns and walks away.

I look around at my room. I guess there's no getting out of this one. This is what I needed, after all. A break from the mundane routine that I'd put myself in.

The flight from Pittsburgh to San Diego was long and stuffy. Seven hours crammed in between some annoying guy on his phone, arguing in another language and a guy who smelled like farts. When I land at San Diego International, I can't wait to get off the plane. I grab my carry on and wait in the line of people shuffling off the plane. When I get out into the clearing, my eyes search for Ava.

"*Violet!*" I hear her scream. My head snaps in the direction that I heard her voice. I find Ava easily, she's wearing a bikini top, a plastic flower lay, cut off shorts and a giant blinking crown that says 'bride'. My jaw drops at the sight of her because she looks like she already got started on her drinking for the night. She waves frantically at me, I spot the rest of the crew behind her. Marie, Ava's big sister, Kate, our mutual friend from high school, Fiona, Ava's cousin and a few other girls that Ava met in college. I walk over to join them and Ava squeezes my neck, nearly choking me. Then she stands back and looks me up and down.

"What? I'm wearing traveling clothes," I defend myself.

"Well I hope you packed 'getting some' clothes, because you're going to be getting some tonight!" she giggles.

I blush, she *definitely* started the party early. There's a limo waiting for us outside, we all load into it, making our way to the hotel we'll be staying in. I admire the palm trees and glimpses of the ocean on our way. *I can't believe I'm finally going to see the ocean*, I think. All of the girls are laughing and being loud while I sit, shyly. Ava pops the champagne in the limo and serves us all a glass.

I decide maybe I should make the first toast, since I'm the maid of honor and all. I raise my glass. "To Ava getting married!"

Everyone cheers and then her sister makes her own toast. "To Ava and Michael!"

We all say, "hip, hip, hooray."

The other girls get so excited that they decide to make *their* own toasts.

"To seeing male strippers!" Fiona yells. We all laugh.

Then Ava decides to make a toast of *her* own. "To Violet losing her virginity!" she shouts.

Everyone gasps and looks at me, I turn red as the bowl of strawberries in the limo. Then they all giggle and Ava cringes, then mouths "sorry" to me. I shrug it off.

We pull up to The Pacific Beach Hotel, I get out and stretch, gratefully. I immediately notice the cool, ocean breeze and the smell of salt in the air. I inhale it deeply, committing it to my memory. I can see the beach from here, the hotel has an ocean view. The sun is beginning to set and all I want to do is drop everything and kick off my sandals and run to the beach like a crazy person, so I do. The other girls, noticing my excitement, follow my lead. If they weren't in a frenzy before, then they certainly are now. We kick up water at each other and scream at how cold it is. Ava is laughing the hardest. After a few minutes, we're cold and wet and hungry, so we all go back to pick up our things that are littered all over the ground. To onlookers, we probably looked like a crazy bunch. We all head into the hotel and are immediately impressed with the cool, beachy feel and decor. It's modern but simple, the furnishings are in blue, white and tan colors. We pass an upscale seafood restaurant inside the hotel and a dark, intimate bar. The elevator we ride in has glass doors and we can see the ocean from it also. We're staying in the presidential suite, at the top of the hotel. We open the door and gasp as we take in everything the room has to offer. There's three rooms with two king sized beds in each room, all the rooms have balconies and ocean views. There's also a living room and kitchen area. All of us girls, very maturely, run into the bedrooms, claiming whose is whose. I end up in the room with Fiona, the crazy one. After a lot of squealing and giggling and shenanigans, we all start getting ready for the evening's festivities. I put jeans and a t-shirt, my usual choice of clothing. Everyone else is wearing short dresses and heels. They primp and fluff, flat iron and spray, while I read a book, waiting.

"What the *hell* are you wearing?" I look up, startled, to see Ava glaring down at me.

"*Clothes*," I raise my brow at her.

She shakes her head. "*Not* those."

I make a face. "Why not?"

"Violet," she scolds, hand on her hip. "We're in *California*, not Pennsylvania."

I sigh. "Well, what did you have in mind?"

Ava smiles wickedly and I gulp.

CHAPTER THREE

Handsome Stranger

I stare at my reflection in the full body mirror in the hotel bathroom. "This is too much," I complain.

I'm wearing a short, sparkly, sapphire dress and nude heels that are way too tall for me. My hair has been curled, teased and pinned up. Ava also did my makeup and successfully achieved the unachievable smoky eye. I don't look *bad*, but I also don't recognize myself.

"It's *not* too much. Quit fussing over yourself, we don't have time to anyway, the car is here to pick us up," she says, her eyes glued to her phone.

I sigh and grab my purse. We all head back down to the limo. I follow behind the herd of girls, feeling not quite as thrilled as they are. I climb in the limo awkwardly, trying not to show my underwear. How do girls *do* this? We drive to a fancy restaurant called Ocean Front, that's only a few miles away from our hotel. Afterwards, we planned to hit up the strip club. We all get out of the limo, causing quite a scene in our short, sparkly dresses and not to mention, most of the girls are already inebriated. We're seated at a long rectangular table. We immediately are served with drinks and hors d'ouevre's. I decide to stick to beer for the night, knowing my alcohol intolerance. Sometime during dinner, I have to pee. I get up too fast and realize quickly that I've already drank too much. I wobble a little, but luckily nobody notices. I walk through the dimly lit restaurant, gazing at the sun setting over the ocean through the windows. For some reason, I can't take my eyes off of the beautiful sight. Not looking where I'm going, I foolishly run into someone. It feels like I've hit a brick wall.

"I'm sorry," I apologize immediately. I look up to see who I've ran into and my mouth drops slightly.

"It's okay. Are you alright?" The handsome stranger smiles. His white teeth gleam against his tan skin. He's tall and wearing a charcoal colored suit. His dark hair is slicked back and his eyes, which are a color that I can't name, twinkle at me.

"Er— yes, thank you," I mumble, embarrassed.

He nods. "Good."

"Nice suit," I blurt out, stupidly. Where did that even *come* from? *Nice suit?* Like I would even *know!* Stupid low alcohol intolerance!

He laughs. "Thank you. Nice *dress*," his eyes roam over it. My cheeks burn hot.

"Xavier Daniels, entrepreneur," he extends his hand.

"Violet Crenshaw, maid of honor." I take his hand in mine, instantly regretting it. His hand is warm and strong and a tingle runs through my body.

He releases my hand and laughs. "*That's* your occupation?"

I get mad, abruptly. "*No*, that's why I'm in California. It was nice meeting you Mr. Daniels, now I have to get back to my very drunk entourage." I turn, trying to exit gracefully, but stumble. I keep walking anyway, not daring to turn around, even though I think I heard him laughing behind me. I make it to the restroom and poke my head back out, making sure he's not around before heading back to my table.

By the time I make it back, everyone's ready to leave. "Vi— where *were* you? I almost sent out the s- search party," Ava slurs, giggling.

My buzz has inconveniently wore off. We all pile back into the limo and head to the strip club. I'm not the most comfortable with the idea, so I decide to have some more champagne in the limo to ease my nerves. We pull up to the place and it's named aptly,

"Dirty Little Secrets." We go inside into the darkly lit club. There's red and pink spotlights everywhere, under each one is a different guy, wearing sparkly thongs. I'm already blushing and we haven't even sat down. We're led to our "private" table and served drinks immediately. The music starts and out come the men. Everyone starts "woo-ing" again, but no one more than the bride herself, who's getting grinded on by two guys at the same time. A blonde guy with slicked back hair makes his way over to me and starts his moves. I cover my face as all the girls cheer. He uncovers my eyes and puts my hands on his overly oiled, muscular chest. My little entourage is almost rabid by then. I try to look anywhere but at the glittery thong he keeps trying to shove into my face. When he finally moves from me to Fiona, I sigh with relief. Fiona cheers and enjoys every moment. I use my cocktail napkins to try to wipe off the oil.

A few hours later, all the girls stumble out of the strip club, looking for more trouble. My buzz has wore off again and I feel dirty, and in desperate need of a shower. We decide to go to a night club down the way from our hotel. The bouncer, seeing a lot of drunk attractive girls, lets us pass the line. Once we're inside, the loud bumping music and flashing lights makes me dizzy. Everyone is dancing in the middle of the floor. I dance with them for a while. I even dance with a few guys, before I get bored. I'm trying to have fun, I *really* am, it just takes a lot more to impress me. I make my way over to Ava, and yell in her ear. *"I'm going outside for a minute."*

She makes a pouty face at me. "Let's keep dancing!" she suggests.

"Ava, my feet are *killing* me," I complain. She nods, understanding. "I'll be back in a few," I promise her.

I head outside, pass the bouncer and go to the back of the club. I had seen some more private looking tables outside and what looked like a bar. The setting there is more quiet and intimate, away from the madness of the club. I walk up the steps and onto the wood covered porch. Heating lamps are lit and there are wooden picnic bench style tables with umbrellas. But the best part is the front and center view of the ocean at night, it's breathtaking, to say the least. I sit down at one of the tables, appreciating how empty it is, there are only a couple of people out here. I text Ava, so she won't worry.

I'm out back, much quieter out here.

I sit for a moment, just gazing at the dark water, watching the couples, walking hand in hand, taking moonlight strolls. The beach air is cool and fresh, I'm grateful for the outdoor heaters, I breathe in deeply. *I wish I was brave enough to let myself fall in love*, I think, idly, watching the couples with jealousy for a moment. I'm about to get up and order a drink when I hear a deep voice beside me.

15

"Alone again?" Xavier Daniels smiles down at me, two drinks in his hands.

I flush, grateful that he can't tell in the night. "What are you *stalking* me, now?" I accuse him, not annoyed one bit.

He laughs. "As much as I'd like to *pretend* I'm that creative, no, I'm not stalking you. This is my club," he raises a brow at me.

I blink. "Your *club?*"

"Yes, I told you I was an entrepreneur, this is one of my businesses," he calmly informs me.

"Oh," I say, surprised, not missing the fact that he said *one* of his businesses.

"Drink?" he offers, setting down one of the glasses he's holding in front of me.

"Sure," I say, still distracted by the fact that he owns this club. *He could be lying...*

He sits without asking permission. "So, what are you like the worst maid of honor ever, or what?" he winks, teasing me.

My mouth drops. "What is that supposed to mean?"

He takes a drink and narrows his eyes at me. "Aren't you supposed to be bride-sitting or something?"

"Bride-sitting?" I raise my brow.

"Yeah," he continues. "You know, making sure she doesn't cheat on her husband to be or whatever."

I scoff. "She'd *never* do that."

"Why are you so sure?" he tests me.

"Because I *know* her, she's head over heels with Michael," I state, like it's a known fact.

He shrugs. "Love isn't everything."

My mouth drops, *where does this guy get off*...but my train of thought is cut off, when I feel him run his fingertips on the top of my hand, softly. "It is nice to keep running into you, though, errant maid of honor or not," he smiles crookedly in the dim light.

I strain for my voice to come out, as I slowly withdraw my hand. He smiles as I do.

"Yes, *why* is it that we only run into each other in dark places? Do you *only* lurk in the shadows?"

That makes him laugh. "I prefer the night, but if you're asking if I come out in the daylight, then yes I do, I'm not a vampire."

I sip the drink cautiously, realizing it's delicious, with hints of spice and fruit. I become suddenly alarmed, remembering that I should never accept a drink from strangers. *Especially* very handsome ones, who lurk at night. "Did you roofie this?" I ask him straight out, I'd never been great at subtlety.

His eyes grow wide and he chokes on his drink. "You aren't *serious?*" he laughs. I stand my ground, waiting.

"*Wow*, you *are* serious. No I didn't 'roofie' that drink. If I wanted to sleep with you, I wouldn't need to *drug* you," he smirks, suddenly over confident.

My face flames once again, I look away. "Where did you say you were from again?" he pries.

"I didn't."

Ava and the crew all stumble out to the back patio bar, where we're sitting. "*There* she is!" she shouts. I couldn't feel more relieved to see her. I get up, ready to join them.

"Until next time?" he asks, looking slightly disappointed.

"I doubt it, thanks for the drink." I slip a twenty on the table, turn and walk away, leaving him alone, and feeling more proud of my exit this time.

He Loves Me...

CHAPTER FOUR

The Wedding

We all pile back into the limo, finally ready to turn in for the night. I wait my turn for the shower, grateful to wash off the dirty smell of cigarette smoke and alcohol, mixed with the scent of man. Not in a good way either. More like in a dirty, male stripper, way. I also can't wait to wash off all of the caked on makeup and hairspray. I don't usually wear all of that, it feels like I'm trying too hard. Most of the girls are already passed out, including Ava, who's snuggling her pillow, drooling with her mouth open. I smile down at her, *I can't believe my best friend is getting married*, I think.

The next day is complete chaos. I wake up to the sound of Ava vomiting in the bathroom. I roll over and rub my eyes, reaching for my phone on the night stand, I notice that it's already 11 a.m. The wedding is at 1 p.m. and we *all* slept in!

"Shit!" I mumble.

I get sleepily to my feet and go to help Ava. On my way, I shake awake the other girls who are scattered everywhere.

I finally get to the bathroom. "Ava, *honey*, you *alright?*" I ask, nervously, moving her hair from her face.

"Mmmm," is all she has to offer. The smell emanating from the toilet overwhelms me and I have to hold my breath. "I know a bride who has to go snag herself a groom today, do you know who that is?" I ask with forced cheer.

That seems to get her attention because she lifts her head up and smiles. "*Me!*" She thrusts one of her fists into the air, victoriously.

"*Yay!* It's *you!* C'mon now, let's get up so we can go get beautiful!" I encourage.

I start trying to lift her off of the toilet, but she flips over and laughs, landing on the floor. "Here comes the bride!" she sings.

"*Fiona!*" I yell. "I could use some *help* here!"

After we all drag of our sorry, hungover asses out of the hotel room and into the salon, we actually resemble a wedding party. I don't know how the makeup artist managed to cover the bags under our eyes. Or how the hairstylist managed to take Ava's tangled, thrown-up in hair and mold and shape it into something breathtaking, but they do. We leave the salon and head back to the hotel to change into our dresses. They're strapless and a dusty rose color, we all wear nude sandals to match. Ava knew the heels wouldn't work in sand, but thought barefoot was too trashy. As Ava makes her way out of her bedroom, I gasp. Her satin white dress hugs her curvy body perfectly. Her hair is piled up in curls atop of her head. Her veil sprouts out of a diamond tiara.

She's grins at me, radiantly. "What do you think?"

"I think Michael's a lucky guy," I smile. "You're *perfection*, Ava."

She looks teary-eyed for a moment. "Thank you. Now let's get out of here before he changes his mind," she laughs.

She holds her out hand to mine, I take it and we make our way to the elevators.

The wedding was definitely one for the books. The weather was perfect and everything went as planned. It was directly on the beach, sand and all. I don't think Ava could've asked for a *more* perfect wedding. Afterwards, we all headed to the reception in the hotel. A room was reserved solely for our wedding party. I was watching Ava, dancing with her new groom, wondering when would I find *my* someone. I had downed a few too many glasses of champagne, when I heard a familiar voice.

"Maid of honor, we meet again."

You've got to be kidding me.

I turn to see none other than Xavier Daniels, standing next to my table. He's dressed sharply in a tan colored suit, with a light blue undershirt. He's not wearing a tie, instead the collar of his shirt is opened, exposing a peek of his tan skin and a smatter of golden chest hair. "Care to dance?" he holds out his hand.

"Care to tell me why you're *here?*" I quip.

"I will if you dance with me," he smiles.

"Sure..." I scoff.

"Pinky promise," he smirks, holding up his pinky.

I try to remain skeptical but accidentally burst into laughter. "I can't believe you just *said* that."

He laughs. "Well, will you or not?"

"Fine," I complain and hold up my pinky.

The moment the word is out of my mouth he pulls me up by the hand and presses me against him, much too close for comfort. "A 'yes' would've been better, but I'll take it," he grins wickedly, before curling his pinky around my own.

My mouth goes dry, the instant reaction I get to our bodies touching is disturbing to me. He holds me close as we sway, all the while staring into my eyes. Elvis Presley's "Falling In Love With You" floats through the air.

"Where'd you learn to dance?" I ask, immediately regretting fluffing his already too fluffed ego.

"Oh, you know, here and there," he winks. The lights twinkle in his eyes, which close up, look to be some sort of golden, hazel color. They confuse the hell out of me.

"So...we're *dancing*, now tell me why you're here," I demand, reminding myself not to get caught up in the feel of his strong arms and how intoxicating he smells.

"Well, truth be told, your friend asked me to come," he whispers, conspiratorially.

My face shows my betrayal. "*Who?*" I look around me.

"*Well*, I don't want to name any names but....she *may* be dancing center stage right now. But who could blame her? It's kind of *her* day," he smirks, directing his gaze at Ava.

"*Ava* asked you to come here?" I gasp.

He twirls me, then holds me fast in his arms, my back pressed to his front. "Admit it, you have more fun when I'm around," he teases, muttering in my ear.

Chills run up my spine. "I don't know if I would describe it as 'fun'," I argue. But the truth is, I was boring my eyes out before he got here.

"What would you call it then?" he turns me back to face him, waiting for my answer.

"Just shut up and dance with me," I blurt out, in annoyance.

He chuckles. "Yes ma'am."

After we dance, I realize I should probably make my maid-of-honor speech. I'd rather Xavier not be here to watch me *do* it, but I have to do it, all the same. I stand, pick up my champagne glass and a fork and clink it to the side of the glass. The crowd goes silent and all eyes land on me. *Great*, public speaking, my worst nightmare. Ava's cousin, Fiona, walks over and hands me the mic. I clear my throat, awkwardly. I glance down at Xavier for a second, quickly wishing I hadn't. He's sitting, watching me, his eyes gleaming with entertainment. Embarrassment heats my body as I start my speech.

"Ava and I have been friends for years. We've done almost everything together since we were little. From matching lunch boxes, to dance classes, which we both know I was terrible at," I laugh and so does the crowd. "We got our first perms together, I think we can *both* agree that was a bad decision," everyone laughs again. "From our first boyfriend's to graduation, we've been there for each other. She was there for me, when my mom passed away...I'll never forget that," I gaze at her across the room, emotion suddenly overcoming me. Everyone is silent a moment, too silent. I'm afraid to look down at Xavier, now. Ava smiles at me, encouragingly. I continue, trying to push the sadness out of my voice. "So when she told me she was going to marry Michael, I couldn't be *happier* for her. She's an amazing person and she deserves someone *equally* amazing. Michael, I think you've made the cut," I chuckle, directing my gaze at the groom. Him and the crowd laugh along with me. Xavier is grinning at me, with admiration. "Ava, you're my best friend, thank you for giving me the 'honor', pun intended." She laughs and shouts. *"You're welcome!"* The crowd breaks into applause. "Seriously though, congratulations to you both!" I raise my glass, everyone in the room follows suit. "To a lifetime of happiness." Everyone repeats the words. "To Ava and Michael!" Everyone clinks their glasses together. I smile at Ava and she beams back at me.

I sit back down and Xavier reaches over to clink his glass to mine. "Not bad, maid of honor," he smirks.

I shrug. "Could've gone worse." To be honest, I was pretty proud of myself for not messing that up. Especially in front of Xavier.

"Go out with me tomorrow," he says, suddenly.

"What?" I ask, still distracted from my speech.

"*What?* Your maid of honor duties are over. You're allowed to have fun now," he winks.

"Um..."

"Oh, come on, don't do that," he grins.

"Do what?"

"Look for an excuse to not go out with me," he raises his brows, knowingly.

I flush, wildly.

"C'mon, a little fun never killed anyone," he gazes into my eyes, flashing me a bright smile.

I sigh. "Alright, where are we going then?" I relent. He's just too damn good looking to turn down.

"It's a surprise," he smiles, entertained. "Meet me on the beach in front of the hotel, tomorrow morning, around 10 a.m."

CHAPTER FIVE

Catalina Island

Ava left to go on her honeymoon last night, in the Bahamas. We had the hotel room for one more night. The next morning, I get up early to get ready for my date with Xavier. My stomach is full of butterflies, I can't believe I'm doing this. It's been years since I've even been on a date.

"Look who's getting all spiffed up." I hear Fiona say, sleepily. I turn to look at her, her eyes are barely squinted open.

"Yeah, I have a date," I smile, nervously, smoothing my wrinkled top.

"*Rawrrrrr*...." she growls at me.

My cheeks heat immediately. "Shut up, Fiona," I laugh.

"Is he hot?" she smiles.

"Ridiculously," I sigh.

"What's his name?" she inquires.

"Xavier," I say.

"He sounds hot," she grins. "Good luck," she yawns and turns back over, going back to sleep.

"Thanks," I mutter.

Ten minutes later, I'm waiting on the beach. I feel like he's not going to show, I don't see anyone. Suddenly, I hear a loud boat horn, I turn in the direction it came from. There's a dock to the left, and a yacht is pulled up to it. I spot a figure standing on the deck, the person is waving...at *me!* I look harder and make out the figure, it's Xavier!

"He has a *yacht?*" I mutter to myself, in disbelief.

I wave back and walk towards the dock. When I reach it, he makes his way back off of the yacht and walks towards me, meeting me on the wooden dock. He walks up to me, smirking mischievously. He looks ultra handsome, in linen boat shorts and a white, short sleeve button up, with only one button actually buttoned. Most of his chest and stomach are exposed, displaying his tan and perfectly chiseled body. His hair is gel free this time and blowing in the breeze.

He flashes me a bright smile. "Surprised?"

I laugh. "You could say that." I squint my eyes and hold my hand up to shield my eyes from the sun.

He holds his hand out to me. "Come on," he urges. I take it and feel tingles run through my own hand as he intertwines our fingers together. We walk the short distance to his yacht. I see the word "Trinity" written on the side. I furrow my brows, wondering why he would name his boat that? Maybe he's actually married? What if he is and that's his *wife's* name? I feel horror building inside of me. Or he could have a daughter? Maybe it was his mother's name? *I have to know the answer before I set foot on this boat*, I think suddenly.

"Why'd you name your boat 'Trinity'?" I ask.

He laughs. "I didn't name it that, I bought it last year from its previous owner. I was going to rename it but it seemed to fit the boat well," he smiles.

"Oh," I say, feeling kind of silly about where my thoughts were headed. I can be very untrusting of people, naturally. A kind of defense mechanism I'd built for myself after my mother died. I stare at the boat with a new fear building.

Xavier seems to pick up on it. "Have you ever been on a boat before?" he inquires, staring at me.

"Um, not really," I admit.

He laughs. "Well, looks like today is your lucky day. The weather is going to be perfect. I hope you wore your swimsuit."

I did wear my bathing suit, but I assumed it would be on the beach with plenty of other people around. I never imagined I would be wearing it for Xavier's eyes only. The thought of his eyes closely scrutinizing my body made me feel shy, suddenly.

Xavier mistakes my moment of inner girly turmoil as me actually not having a suit. "It's no problem if you didn't, I bought one for you in case," he reassures me.

"You *bought* me a bathing suit?" I ask, even more surprised. He nods.

"But you don't know my *size*," I argue, my cheeks heating.

He shrugs. "I can guess," he smirks.

For some reason, I *really* want to see the bathing suit he bought me, but I decline. "That's okay, I have mine on underneath," I say.

"Good," he smiles. "Let's go then." He steps onto the deck.

I pause for a moment, a flicker of intuition running through me. I'm getting on a boat with a *stranger*, I think. Is this actually a *smart* decision? Of course I'm trying to talk myself out of this, that's what the *old* Violet would do. I'm supposed to be having *fun*, getting on a boat would be fun, *right? Especially* a yacht. Only one way to find out, I decide. I step onto the deck, feeling excited. At least I told *Fiona* who I was with. I know she's not the most *reliable* source, but if someone wants to know, she'll tell them. That bit of information gives me a little sense of relief, enough to have fun for today at least.

He unties the boat and we start to float away from the deck, slowly. He turns to me, "you can swim, right?" he teases.

"Of course I can swim," I scoff.

Thirty minutes later, we're farther away from the shore. I watch it grow smaller and smaller. "Where are we going?" I wonder, nervously.

Xavier, who's steering the boat turns and smiles at me through his aviator sunglasses. "Catalina Island"

Of course I haven't heard of it, so there's not much to say, so I just nod. Sounds nice, I've never been to an island, either. I'm sure he knows that, too. "How much longer 'til we get there?" I ask. I didn't plan on going to an *island* today. But I guess I didn't plan on getting on a yacht today, either.

"Twenty minutes," he shouts.

I nod, my hair whipping back in the cool, ocean breeze. A little while later, we turn a corner of the island, and I see it finally come into view. It's beautiful actually, despite it's charming size. It's made up of jagged rocks, lush greenery and small, colorful houses littering the hills. Xavier points and I look in the direction. Dolphins are jumping in the waves on either side of the boat. I'd definitely never seen dolphins before. My mouth drops. "Oh my gosh," I smile hugely. "They're so cute!" Xavier laughs.

Ten minutes later, we're pulling up to a boat docking area. Xavier "parks" the boat and ties it up. "Hungry?" he asks.

"Yes," I laugh.

"Good, I know this great place," he says, taking my hand and leading me off the boat.

We eat at small seafood restaurant, overlooking the ocean. Our conversation flows easily enough. I find out that Xavier is 25, only three years older than me. He was an only child and grew up in Florida, his parents are both retired and still live there. He decided to try life out on the west coast and studied business in college. I tell him about my life, leaving a big gap about my mom's passing. I know he already knows about it, because of the wedding, but I don't want to ruin the mood of our date. After we eat, Xavier gets a playful twinkle in his eye. "Ready for another adventure?"

I eye him, warily. "Depends."

He laughs a hearty laugh. "You really need to learn to have fun."

I playfully shove him on the shoulder, accidentally feeling his bulging muscles in the process. We take a taxi to the other side of the island and when we pull up, I feel more unease when I find out what he's brought me to do. A large sign reads "*Parasailing $50* " I spot several bright, rainbow-colored parachutes attached to boats in the distance. The people in the parachutes look like tiny dots in comparison to the parachutes and boats. We get out of the car and Xavier pays the cabbie. I stand, waiting, wishing I had an excuse to get me out of this. Xavier turns to me faster than I would've liked. "Ready?" he smirks. My mouth dries up and my eyes widen in alarm. Xavier seems to find my reaction very entertaining, he laughs. "Come on, you'll be fine."

We walk up to sign the waivers and pay. When there's a boat and driver available, we climb in. After we have our life vests on and are given our rules, I'm ten times more nervous.

"You two ready?" Our driver, named Gary asks.

I nod and Xavier laughs again. "Yes, we're ready," he answers.

The parachutes are prepared and we get into our harnesses. Gary gives us the countdown. My heart is thumping slowly in my chest. Right before he gets to one, Xavier grabs my hand. I look over at him and he's smiling at me, warmly. Then we're released. My heart falls into my stomach as we rise higher and higher into the air. A scream of delight escapes my lips. I look below us, our feet are dangling feet above the ocean. My hair is blowing in the breeze. The sun is warm on my skin. I can see almost the whole island. I almost forget Xavier is with me, until he speaks up.

"Not so bad, huh?" he asks, knowingly.

I turn to him, an ecstatic grin on my face. "I'm having so much fun, Xavier, thank you."

"Date's not over yet," he winks at me.

CHAPTER SIX

House Guest

After parasailing, we were hungry again. We take another taxi, winding up a road on the top of the island.

"Where are we going now, Xavier?" I wonder aloud.

He just smiles. "Somewhere special to me," he reaches over and grabs my hand.

I almost withdraw it, but I don't want to be rude, so I don't. He holds it until we pull up beside a house. It's a quaint, little beach house, but it's absolutely adorable. I look at Xavier, but he's busy paying the cabbie. He gets out and opens the door for me and I climb out, confused. "What's this?" I ask. "Another restaurant?"

Xavier chuckles. "No, this is my house."

"You live...*here?* On the *island?*" I ask, confounded.

"Yes, well, I have few houses," he explains.

"Oh...." A *few?*

He holds his hand out to me. "Come on, I'm going to make you dinner," he smiles.

Make me dinner? I've never had a guy do *that* for me. I notice the sun is setting, does he expect me to stay the night? Are boats allowed to sail across at night? Is it *safe?* I have to stop right there. Here, I have this super handsome guy, who's taken me on his yacht, bought me lunch, taken me parasailing and wants to cook me dinner, and I'm trying to talk myself *out* of it? I shake my head a little and walk to him, smiling and place my hand in his.

We walk inside and it's just as adorable on the inside. Cozy and beachy, I'm relieved it doesn't have "bachelor pad" written all over it. "This is nice," I compliment him.

"Thanks," he smiles. "I hope you like shrimp linguini," he says.

My mouth practically waters at the mention of it. "That sounds delicious," I nod.

As he starts to get the ingredients out of his fridge, I wander to the glass windows on the opposite side of the house. I walk up to them and peer out. The view overlooks most of the island and the beach. "Wow, the view you have here is....*wow*," I say.

He smirks and shrugs while sautéing the shrimp. "It's not bad."

"How long have you had this place?" I walk back over to him, watching him cook. For some reason, he looks even *more* attractive when he does, if that's even possible.

"Only a year," he answers. "I actually used to live in Greece," he says, thoughtfully.

"*Greece?*" I squeak. Does he *know* that's one of my dream places to go? Did he read my mind or something?

He turns to look at me, confused by my tone and expression. "Yeah, I still haven't sold the home I own there. I'm attached to it, I think about going back all the time."

Inside, I'm reeling. I want to scream, 'please take me!!!' But I know how desperate that would sound and how awkward of a position I'd be putting him in.

"Greece... is beautiful," I say instead.

"Oh, you've been?" he asks, as he plops one of the shrimp into his mouth, sucking his fingers afterward.

I'm immediately distracted by the action and have to force my eyes back upward to look into his. "Uh...um...no. I've just, heard. You know..." I mumble like a fool, barely managing to speak coherently.

"Oh. Well, you should go. I can take you?" he offers.

For a split second, my wayward thoughts take me in the wrong direction. He's watching me though, waiting. My cheeks flush at the thought. *If only he could read my mind.* "Oh! Well, that's very nice of you. But, no...I couldn't do that," I breathe.

"Well, sure you can!" he enthuses. "All you need is a passport," he says, like it's no big deal.

"Oh. Well, maybe then," I laugh, awkwardly. Is he *serious?* What world does this guy *live* in?

"Good, I'll start making plans to arrange it," he smiles, winningly. *What?!?* "But for now," he smiles, "bon appétit!" He sets a plate of steaming hot linguini under my nose. The aroma is simply mouthwatering. The boy knows how to cook.

We eat dinner outside on his back patio overlooking the island. "More wine?" he asks, refilling my glass before I agree. I want to say no, but the wine is delicious, pink, sweet and bubbly. I can feel the heavy feeling in my limbs, I'm already getting tipsy.

"Thanks. Do you usually drink pink wine?" I tease.

He smirks. "No, I bought this one for *you*."

"Oh..."

He must've really planned this all out. I can't help but be flattered. When we get done, I think he's going to take me back, finally. But instead he leads me to another part of his back patio. I follow, with butterflies in my stomach. My jaw drops when I spot the jacuzzi, with an even more stunning view of the ocean.

"Want to get in?" he asks, smiling like he already knows the answer. He unbuttons the lone button that was holding his shirt together and I'm forced to stare at all of his perfectly tan and sculpted upper body. He climbs in and rests his head back on the edge of the jacuzzi. "Ah," he smiles, lazily. "Your turn," he waits, watching.

My mouth drops for an instant. Great. This is exactly what I was afraid of, a moment like this. I know my body isn't terrible, but compared to him, I'm out of shape. I feel excruciatingly shy anytime I have to expose skin. I gather my composure before unbuttoning my shorts and shimmying them off. I look up and Xavier's watching me, studying my every move. The expression on his face makes my knees weak. I'm even more nervous than before. I smile, weakly at him and quickly remove my tank top, roughly pulling it over my head. I climb in the jacuzzi quickly, trying to hide my body as fast as I can. I feel clumsy and weak from the wine, I hope he didn't notice that I almost stumbled.

Xavier stares at me, from across the jacuzzi, a mixture of curiosity and amusement written on his features. He moves over to sit next to me. "You shouldn't be ashamed of your body, it's beautiful," he murmurs. I feel overwhelmingly hot suddenly, I don't know if it's the jacuzzi or Xavier's direct words, that causes it. Maybe it's a combination of the two.

"Thank you," I mutter, not wanting to meet his eyes.

As if knowing I don't want to look at him, he lifts my chin and forces me to. "That bathing suit matches your eyes," he compliments me further.

I smile a little. "Blue is my favorite color," I explain, suddenly glad that I chose to wear the cobalt-colored bikini.

He leans forward. "I think it's mine, too," he smiles, staring at my lips. My heartbeat picks up pace. He licks his lips, and I feel like I may pass out if he kisses me. I'm about to object, but as soon as I open my mouth, he goes in for the kill. He parts my lips with his tongue, causing me to gasp, involuntarily. My reaction only seems to encourage him more. He slips his hand behind my neck, holding me in place. Before I know it, I'm kissing him back like a hormonal teenager. He tugs at my hair, gently, tilting my head backwards, granting himself access to my neck. I've kissed a few boys in my day, but it's nothing like kissing Xavier. He's *too* smooth and *too* good. He kisses like a bad boy, a very, *very* bad boy.

He releases me, staring into my eyes, with intensity. "Spend the night with me, Violet," he pleads.

CHAPTER SEVEN

Cruel Intentions

That question sobers me faster than anything. My heart thumps slow and loud in my chest. "What?" I ask stupidly, thinking I must've heard him wrong. But deep down inside, I know I didn't, I just need to buy myself more time to respond.

"Spend the night with me, Violet," he repeats, this time with more conviction.

Somehow the stalling did me no good at all, because I'm still at a loss for words. "I...I..." I stutter. He keeps staring at me with his gold eyes and soft, kissable lips.....

"You're thinking too hard," he smiles at me fondly, brushing his thumb across my bottom lip. "You should think less and *feel* more..." his eyes twinkle.

From under the water, I feel his hand on my thigh. He drags his fingertips up and down it slowly, inches away from my bikini line. My skin is hypersensitive and tingly where he touches. My breathing is erratic, and my body temperature skyrockets. My heart is racing fast, too fast. It's too much, too soon. I know I told myself I was going to let loose and have fun, but this was moving too fast. Even with a perfect, gorgeous man like Xavier.

I jump up suddenly. "I'm hot," I blurt out.

Xavier's mouth hangs open slightly, in surprise. "Yes, you *are*," he recovers, smiling.

"No," I breathe. "That's not what I meant. I want to get out of the jacuzzi," I clarify.

Xavier looks slightly disappointed but just nods. He climbs out and I want to punch myself when I see the way he looks when he's wet. *Maybe it's not too late to change my mind? No!* I already decided. I follow after him, trying not to stare.

He hands me a towel. I wrap myself in it, quickly. "Do you have a boyfriend?" he asks, his eyes narrowed with suspicion.

"No," I sigh. "I just...we barely know each other. I've never done this kind of thing before..." I try to explain.

He wraps the towel around his waist. "What? A one night stand? Is *that* what you thought this was?" he sounds offended.

"Yes, I mean *no*. I mean, I've never actually, um...never mind," I stumble over my words, mortified of what I almost just admitted. *What is wrong with me?*

He stares at me, furrowing his brows for a moment, but then he suddenly looks serious. Realization dawns on him. "You're a *virgin?*" he asks, astonished.

"No," I blurt out, immediately. He *can't* know that. I would be beyond embarrassed. "I mean, I'm twenty-two, come on," I laugh, trying to play it off.

He scrutinizes my face for a moment, but then decides to let it go. "Come on, I'll make you some coffee," he offers.

Once we're inside, and wearing clothes again, I feel a little calmer. I sip the coffee he made me, feeling slightly embarrassed for panicking. "I've had a lot of fun today." I try to bring back the lighthearted mood we had earlier.

"Good," he nods. There's an awkward silence. I guess I wounded his ego. I didn't know that was *possible* when you looked like *that.*

"I thought we were just going to go swimming at the beach," I laugh, confessing. "You really surprised me."

"Swimming at the beach, that's so...*predictable*," he smirks, his confidence peeking through again. "*Any* guy could take you to do that," he scoffs.

I'm about to argue that point, because I wouldn't go out with "any guy" but I let that drop. "And you're not just 'any guy'?" I challenge.

"Definitely not," he winks at me. *There he is.*

I look at my phone, it's 8:30 p.m. As much fun as I'm having with Xavier, I am worried about getting back. I decide to bring it up, carefully. "So what's the plan, now?" I ask.

"I don't know, you want to watch a movie or something?" he asks, smiling at me. "Or would that be too typical?"

"No, that's fine. Are we not going back to San Diego?" I try to act cool about it.

"Not tonight. It's too dark out to sail back now. You can stay the night here, with me. So we can get to know each other better," he grins, his eyes dancing with humor. "You're cool with that, right?" he asks, furrowing his brows.

"Sure, yeah," I answer immediately. Wait, *am I cool with that?* It doesn't go unnoticed by me that he never really gave me a choice.

My phone on the counter between us pings, displaying a message from Fiona. Both of our eyes snap to it at the same time.

How's it going with the hottie? Have you let him de-flower you yet?

My face flames and I snatch my phone up, when our eyes meet I can tell he read the message already. "Excuse me for a moment," I say hurriedly, mortified.

"Certainly," he smirks, pleased with the fact that his guess earlier has just been confirmed.

I walk into the hallway to text Fiona back. I can see his bedroom, the door is open. The bed looks soft and fluffy. I feel my stomach flipping at the possibility of ending up in it, with him.

I type into my phone. *No! Stop texting me. He just read the last one you wrote!*

I can tell she's typing something back and I wait, impatiently. *No shit? Lol sorry.* She writes. I roll my eyes, fully aware that she can't see me. She texts me again. *I might've done you a big favor, though ;)*

I can't deal with Fiona right now. I'm about to walk back when I get another message. I slide my phone over, already irritated, but it's a message from my dad. *Why are you at Catalina Island?*

Oh...this is awkward. I forgot that he "follows" me on "find friends". I try to think of something to write back. *Me and a couple of the girls from the wedding party wanted to go parasailing.*

That was half true, at least. I sigh, heavily. You know your love life is non-existent when your *parents* still check up on you, constantly.

Oh, okay. Be careful. Love you. He writes.

I feel even worse now. *Ok. Love you too, dad.* I text him.

I smack my hand to my face. I have *no* game. How long can I keep pretending to be on Xavier's level? Well, I guess the cat's out of the bag now, anyway. I wonder to myself if that information will scare him off or encourage him? Oh, God, how can I *face* him now? I turn the corner, back into the kitchen and run smack into him. It feels like running into a brick wall again. The wind gets knocked out of me. Xavier puts both of his hands on the top of my shoulders, steadying me.

"Shit, sorry Xavier," I mutter embarrassed, trying to find my breath.

He shakes his head. "*I'm* fine, are *you* okay?" he asks, looking into my eyes.

"Yes, I'm fine," I answer. Damn, his body is all muscle.

He smiles down at me. "Good." He removes his hands from my shoulders and takes my hand in his. "Now how about that movie?" he winks.

I nod. I think we're going to go back into the living room, but instead he leads me into his bedroom. I watch him, feeling like a lamb in the lion's den. He turns on the TV, selects a DVD and slides it in. Funny, I would've pictured him more of a "Netflix" guy. He sits on his bed and pats the spot next to him expectantly, smiling at me irresistibly. I walk over cautiously and sit down next to him. Damn, the bed is soft.

My attention is drawn to the TV when I hear the movie starting. When I realize what it is, I feel like he chose it on purpose. The irony is not lost on me. He picked "Cruel Intentions". Of course I've seen the movie, as have most people my age. It seems all too familiar right now. Wealthy bad boy, tries to corrupt virginal good girl, but falls in love by accident. Was he *trying* to send me a message?

"Cruel Intentions," I nod.

"Have you seen it?" he turns to me, a sparkle in his eye.

"Yes," I answer. The tension in the room is ridiculous. Why is it so *hard* to have a *normal* conversation with him?

"I thought you'd like it," he smirks. He's *totally* doing this on purpose. "Okay," he grins. "I'm all yours, what else do you want to know about me?"

CHAPTER EIGHT

Ferry Ride

I wake up confused. My body feels strange. The bed I'm laying on is far too comfortable, so instead of fighting my eyes open, I let them fall back heavily closed. Powerless, I inhale the scent of the strange, plushy bed for a clue. It smells heavenly, I stretch my limbs and spread them out greedily, savoring the feel of the soft sheets. Suddenly, I detect another scent wafting into my vicinity. *Bacon?* Am I in *heaven?* A deep voice, startles me out of my stupor.

"Good morning, gorgeous. I made you breakfast," he purrs, pleasantly.

My heart stops beating in my chest as I recall just exactly where I am. *Oh, my*....I'm at Xavier's still. My eyes fly open and I turn to stare at him. He's standing next to me, holding a tray with food, wearing only a breathtaking grin, and grey boxer-briefs.

I go to sit up, the sheets slip off of my bare skin and I grab them back immediately, covering myself. I'm *naked?!?* Xavier chuckles. "No need to be shy around me *now*," he teases, winking at me. He sets down the tray in front of me.

"Thank you," I croak, completely befuddled.

He nods. "I'm going to take a shower, enjoy your breakfast," he excuses himself. I watch him walk away, my jaw drops at the sight of his perfect back side. As soon as he leaves, I peek inside the sheets. *Please have my bottoms on, please have my bottoms on*, I hope to myself blindly. Nope. *Oh, my*...I remember now.

It started innocently enough...talking, a movie, a little more wine. Then *lots* more wine, then we got back in the jacuzzi. That's when things heated up. Images start to flash through my mind. The look in Xavier's eyes. Xavier untying my bikini top. Xavier's mouth all over me. Xavier carrying me to his bed. His hands exploring my body. My hands exploring *his* glorious body. Xavier on top of me....

Shit! I slept with him. *More than once!* I can't *believe* I did that! My stomach grumbles and I realize that I should probably eat. I devour the plate of delicious food in front of me. Bacon, potatoes and tortillas. The potatoes are seasoned perfectly. The tortillas taste hand made. He can't be *real*. I finish my plate and down the glass of orange juice. I set the tray aside and go in search of my clothes. I find my bottoms on the floor and pull them on. I realize how incredibly sore *that* area is and gulp to myself. I find my bikini top hanging on the top of the bed and put it on. I can't seem to find my other clothes, so I put on Xavier's t-shirt that I find on the floor. I find my phone on the floor and text Fiona immediately.

SOS! I need someone to come pick me up from Catalina Island ASAP!

I listen to the shower water running as I wait for her response. I look at the time, it's 10:15 a.m. she might still be passed out. But then my phone pings.

Lol I knew it. Just take the ferry you bonehead. If I were you, I wouldn't be running away from THAT though. Are you crazy?

The ferry! I slip on some of Xavier's shorts and find my flip flops. I find a pen and notepad on his bedside table and scribble down a note quickly. *"Thanks for breakfast."* I know that doesn't really describe everything that's happened between us since yesterday too well, but I have no idea what else to write. I feel like it would be just plain rude to not at least thank him for the delicious breakfast he made me. I find my purse in the living room, grab it and walk briskly out of the front door. Xavier lives pretty high up on the island, but luckily a taxi happens to be passing by. I flag it down and climb inside. "Take me to the ferry," I say.

As I'm sailing away from the island, watching it grow smaller in the distance, I start to feel bad. I imagine his face when he walked out of the bathroom and didn't see me. When he saw my pathetic note and probably felt like I didn't even respect him enough to tell him goodbye in person. I sigh, deeply. I'm a terrible person. I realize he doesn't even have my number. *Wow, good job, Violet, a clean break.* He was worried that I thought he wanted a one night stand, but instead I pulled one on him. And for what? *Why was I running?* What was I even running *from?* Maybe people *can't* change. Maybe my heart had been frozen solid. Maybe it was too late for me to love someone new. Tears brim in my eyes. I'm too afraid to let anyone in since my mom died. The loss was too great to me. I *never* wanted to feel it again. But this fear would be my prison. It would trap me and prevent me from moving forward.

"I feel sorry for the asshole *you* ran out on." A deep, rich voice behind me startles me and makes me jump.

I whirl around to see if this stranger is talking to *me.* "He must've been a real dick," the man smiles from underneath his baseball cap. I can't see much of his face as he leans against the wall of the boat. The shadow being cast by his hat, only allows me to see his mouth. His lips are full and sensual, his smile isn't too bad either. *What are you thinking, Violet? You're still wearing another man's clothes!* I internally scold myself for even finding another man attractive at this moment.

"How do you know that I ran out on someone?" I challenge, slightly annoyed that I find him attractive.

"It's kind of obvious," he pulls out a cigarette, sticks it between his lips and lights it.

"Oh really, *how?*"

I cringe at the fact that he smokes, it's such a turn off to me. *See? I'm not attracted to him after all.*

"You're still wearing his *clothes*," he takes a long draw and then blows it out. *Duh, Violet,* I think. *Stop staring at his mouth!* His hands aren't bad either, they look like a man's hands should, strong and rugged.

"You should mind your own business." I mean to sound intimidating but my voice wavers, showing my embarrassment.

"Sorry, I can't help it," he flicks his cigarette away and walks over to stand by me, I feel my wall of defense go up. He lifts his face to finally meet my eyes. "It's kind of my *job*," he smiles. "Detective Soloman Jacobs, pleasure to meet you....?" he trails off, wanting me to tell him my name. I'm too distracted by how handsome he is and how unique *his* name is. His brown eyes are sharp and intelligent, thick brown hair is hidden by his hat.

"Violet Crenshaw," I answer.

"Nice to meet you, Violet," he smiles down at me, warmly.

"You too," I say, still perplexed as to *why* he's talking to me.

"*Violet*...that's a unique name," he notes.

"So is Soloman," I counter and he nods, a small smile playing on his lips.

His expression changes to a more serious one. "Please don't be offended but I have to ask...the man you ran from, he wasn't trying to *hurt* you, was he?" he asks, his eyebrows furrowing in concern.

"What? *No!* Of *course* not," I breathe, half surprised, half embarrassed.

"Okay, good. Just making sure. You looked...like you were afraid or upset or something....that's all. I just wanted to see that you were okay," he explains.

I narrow my eyes at him. "How very *kind* of you. I'm fine, thank you."

"That's good to hear," he smiles at me, unaffected by my bitterness.

We pull up to the dock and the ferry begins to unload. Soloman pulls out a card and hands it to me. "If you ever need help, give me a call," he says. I stare at it and shake my head, wanting to hand it back to him, but he's already walking away.

I sigh and walk off the ferry. "Today has been so *strange*," I say to myself, slipping the card in my bikini top.

I'm about to hail a cab when I hear a car honk. I look over and see Fiona hanging out of the window of a red Ford Focus. She's waving at me frantically. I wave back and make my way over.

"Thanks for picking me up," I breathe.

"No prob, anytime, well, anytime *after* nine a.m. anyway," she jokes. I laugh and we pull away. She turns towards me. "Now tell me *everything*, you little skanky pants," she teases.

I slap her on the arm. "Fiona!" I scold her, but I know it's all in good fun. I tell her most of what happened, leaving out parts that are too personal or embarrassing.

"Damn, girl. Send him my way if you don't want him," she laughs. "Well since you were gone when we checked out of the hotel, I brought your bag in the trunk," she informs me.

"Oh my gosh, thank you. I forgot all about that," I confess. I can't believe Xavier had me so *distracted*. We're all supposed to fly back tomorrow night.

"So where are we staying tonight?" I ask.

"Whatever we can afford," she laughs.

I make a face. "That's not good."

CHAPTER NINE

Run-In

We end up checking into a Motel 6 a few blocks away from our first hotel. It's definitely a downgrade from the presidential suite with a beachfront view at The Pacific Beach Hotel, but it's somewhere to sleep. Marie and Kate checked in and got the adjoining room that connects with ours. I still don't know how I've ended up with crazy cousin Fiona. But I have to admit, she's growing on me. After I shower and change into clean clothes, my stomach grumbles and I realize I haven't ate since this Xavier cooked for me this morning. I flush to myself as I remember how he looked in his boxer-briefs.

"I'm starved," I complain to Fiona.

"Me too," she nods. "Shall we call the rest of the girls and meet for dinner?" she offers.

"Yes," I say, emphatically.

Thirty minutes later we're all eating at In-N-Out Burger. Yet again, not the fanciest place in town, but we were all running low on funds by now. We'd also heard the burgers here were amazing. Fiona is seriously chowing down in front of me, eating with no manners at all. Marie notices and comments. "Fiona, ew, you're disgusting. Close your mouth," she laughs.

"I'm sorry, but this is the best burger I've ate in a while," she says with her mouth stuffed. "I may have another after this," she admits. We laugh at her.

"So where did you *go* last night?" Marie asks. "We missed you when we went out," she adds, innocently. Everyone's staring at me with wide curious eyes, except for Fiona, who's grinning ridiculously at me with food in her mouth.

Marie has always been protective of me, naturally, because she's my best friend's big sister. I'm afraid to admit to anything to her though. Ava would be beyond jealous if I divulged any details to Marie before *her*.

"Umm," I start.

"She went on a date with Xavier," Fiona blurts out. Maybe I spoke too soon about liking her?

My eyes bug out of my head and my mouth drops open in betrayal. "*Fiona!*" I scold.

"What?" She acts like it's no big deal that she just outed me.

They all stare at me, waiting for an explanation. "Who's *Xavier?*" Kate asks, her blue eyes lighting up with curiosity.

I'm about to open my mouth when Fiona answers for me again. "The guy we met at the club the other night, and he was at the wedding," she explains, shoving a handful of fries into her mouth.

"Ohhhh," they both say at the same time.

"He's gorgeous," Kate adds.

"Does *Ava* know?" Marie arches her brow. She looks just like Ava when she looks at me like that. Even though she's a few years older than her, they could be twins, with their tan skin, luscious black hair and piercing green eyes.

"Not yet," I admit. "But it was no big deal, we just went....." They all give me their undivided attention. "Swimming," I finish.

Fiona snorts and I snap my head to hers, shooting her a warning glare. She gets the hint though and shuts up.

"Sounds nice," Marie says and I nod and resume eating, not wanting to discuss it for a moment longer. The other girls all do the same, even loud-mouthed Fiona.

I sigh heavily and look around, not wanting to meet any of their eyes right now. I spot a very handsome guy getting out of a very sharp looking, shiny, black car. I decide to divert my attention to him to distract myself. I watch him walk through the sunlight to the door and open it. Once he's inside, I realize with dread. *"Oh shit,* it's Xavier," I accidentally mutter out loud. *What are the odds?*

"Speak of the devil," Fiona teases.

Three sets of eyes turn his way. "*Where?*" Marie asks.

"Right there," Fiona points. "That stone cold fox right there."

I slap her hand down. "*Stop it!*" I command. "*Don't* look," I duck my head down, pulling down my hat to hide my face.

But their interest is already piqued, they're all gawking shamelessly. "Wait, why are you *hiding*, Vi?" Marie asks. "Did the date go bad?" her eyebrows pull together.

"Sorta," I breathe, feeling like I'm about to have a panic attack. "*Why is he here?*" I mutter to myself.

Fiona, the smart-ass she is, says, "well, *my* guess is he wanted a cheeseburger."

I ignore her. "Are you guys almost done? I *really* want to leave," I plead, trying not to look his way. I'm relieved that it's so packed in here right now. I could slip past him easily without being noticed.

"Actually, *I'm* still eating," Fiona smiles, devilishly. I literally want to punch her in the face.

Luckily, Marie is on my side. "Let's go guys, obviously Violet is uncomfortable," she urges.

We all get up, Fiona reluctantly, and carry our trays, throwing away our scraps of food. I keep my eyes on Xavier the whole time. He's waiting in the never ending "pick-up" line, he should be there for a while. But as we begin to make our way through the crowd, he gets handed his bag of food.

"Why'd *he* get his food so fast?" I complain aloud, the other girls look too.

"Probably because he looks like a model," Fiona says. "He probably likes his burger 'animal style'," she adds, waggling her brows at me.

I don't have time to scold her this time though, because he starts heading towards the door at the same time we are.

"Shit, he's *coming! Hurry!*" Marie pushes me forward.

But so many people are coming in and out that I get lost in the crowd. I end up losing sight of the other girls. Suddenly, I feel a firm hand grasp my shoulder, I whip around to find Xavier staring down at me, looking confused.

"*Violet?*"

Shit.

"Oh hi, Xavier. I didn't see you there," I breathe, breathless at once.

He makes a face like he knows better. "Can we talk outside?" he asks.

I nod and make my way through the door, feeling him right behind me. My stomach flips uncontrollably as I wrack my brain for excuses to make up for leaving so abruptly this morning. Once we're outside in the daylight, facing him makes me all the more nervous. He's dressed more casual than usual, in fitted jeans and a t-shirt. He still looks better than anyone around. In my peripheral vision, I spot the girls watching me in the red Ford Focus. Fiona gives me a thumbs up and I ignore her.

I expect him to be upset. I get ready to apologize, but he surprises me. "I'm having a small get together tonight at my place..." I eye him and he clarifies.

"Here in San Diego. I was going to call you and ask you if you wanted to come, but I don't have your number," he reminds me, smirking.

I don't know how to react, I expected him to say something else entirely. *He doesn't hate me? Maybe this is a trick? What if he wants to get me back?* I stare into his gold eyes, trying to decipher what's behind them. But the more I stare into them, the more I remember from last night. I'm blushing uncontrollably.

He mistakes my hesitation for rejection and says quickly, "you can bring your friends?" he offers, looking worried that I might say no.

I smirk. "Sounds okay," I relent.

I'll show up out of politeness, then tell him that I had the best time ever, and say my goodbyes.

He grins winningly. We exchange numbers. "I'll text you the address and time later," he smiles. Then he leans forward and whispers into my ear, "besides, you left your clothes at my house." Chills run up my spine. He straightens up and slips his aviator sunglasses on, smirking at me. I feel like I'm about to fall over as I watch him get into his shiny Mercedes and drive off.

I walk stiffly to the car and get in, everyone's looking at me of course.

"How'd it go?" Marie asks, looking concerned.

"He invited us all to a party tonight," I answer.

Fiona smiles from the driver's seat. "I hope he has a twin brother," she holds her hands up and pretends to pray.

Just as we're driving away, I get a text message.

5214 Sandy Ave. 7 p.m. Can't wait to see you there ;)

CHAPTER TEN

Party

I look myself up and down in my reflection in the hotel mirror. Fiona lent me an outfit, since all of my clothes were too "virginal" for a "non-virgin" like me. According to Fiona, anyway. Whatever *that* means because I don't *feel* any different. I still feel just as inexperienced as before. I'm wearing a gray, ruffly blouse with a plunging neck line, dipping further down than I'm comfortable with and a short, dark purple skirt.

"I don't really know if this outfit looks like a 'farewell' outfit." I scrunch my nose uncomfortably, peeking at Fiona who's still digging in her suitcase for something.

"What are you *talking* about?" she scoffs. "It's *perfect*. You look super hot in that skirt. He's going to get on his knees and *beg* you to stay!" she says, breathless, struggling with an object in her suitcase.

"But I don't *want* him to." I run my hands through my hair, my cheeks growing hot with frustration. "It would never work! I live in Pennsylvania!" I insist, trying to convince myself more than her.

Fiona is preoccupied with her suitcase though and ignores me. She pulls the object out with her hand, the force of the pull sending her toppling backwards. For a minute, she's a tangle of pale limbs but she recovers and sits back up. *"Got it!"* she exclaims, holding up the leopard print high-heel up high.

"These are for you tonight!" she breathes, smiling victoriously, her red hair falling into her face.

Me, Fiona, Marie, and Kate pull up to Xavier's house and I'd like to say I'm surprised, but it's exactly what I expected. Especially when we started driving higher up, into the streets that hold the huge houses on the hills.

"Nice place," Kate comments, arching a brow.

"That is *way* too much house for one person," I mumble to myself.

My nerves are already causing my hands to shake slightly. I knew I was in too deep the moment I met him, yet I still agreed to take him on. I made my bed, now I have to lie in it, with Xavier apparently. Not that that would be a *bad* thing...? I have no idea how to handle someone like him though, we live in different worlds. *The faster I break things off, the better.* I rehearse to myself, in my head.

We park in the line of cars, littering the long curved driveway. Our car stands out, paling in comparison to all the other shiny, expensive cars, much like Xavier's. We all get out and I suddenly feel under-dressed for the occasion. I pull at my skirt, trying to make it longer. We walk up and ring the doorbell. Xavier swings it open immediately and I lose my breath at the sight of him. He's wearing a black button-up shirt, it fits him well. His muscles are bulging through the thin fabric. He has the top three buttons unbuttoned, exposing a peek of his chest and a gold chain around his neck. He has matching black pants, and dark brown shoes and belt. Black and brown, supposedly colors you shouldn't wear together, but of course Xavier pulls it off like no one else can. His hair is slicked back, leaving his handsome features on full display. I think I can even smell his hypnotic cologne from here. His eyes find mine first, then trail down my body, all the way down to my feet and back up again. He smiles but never takes his eyes off of me as he steps back and holds open the door for us.

"Ladies, do come in. The drinks and food are in the kitchen, help yourselves to anything you want."

He creates a wide berth, letting everyone pass. I'm not sure how I get pushed to the back of the line, but I'm the last one in, granting Xavier his window of opportunity. He holds my elbow as I pass, causing me to pause. He closes the door behind him, still holding onto me.

"Not so fast, gorgeous," he winks at me, playfully. I smile, chagrined. "I need to talk to you," his eyes soften momentarily.

I'm caught off guard by the sincerity of his voice. "Okay," I agree but the coward I am, I add, "can I get a drink first?" I procrastinate.

Xavier looks mildly disappointed but shakes his head. "Of course," he agrees and leads the way to the kitchen.

All of my friends are in the kitchen already, shamelessly helping themselves to the food and booze. The only one who looks slightly hesitant is Marie, she keeps a watchful eye on me. I introduce them all to Xavier.

"Xavier this is Ava's sister, Marie, her cousin, Fiona and Kate." He nods to all of them.

"So," Fiona starts, "Violet tells me you're an only child, what a shame. I was hoping you had a brother," she winks. I feel a blush creeping up my cheeks.

Xavier shakes his head and laughs. "No, I don't have a brother, but I did invite my cousin, Cruz. He's outside by the pool if you want to meet *him*," he suggests.

Fiona looks more than interested, she grabs two beers and waggles her brows at us. "Dibs," she says and makes her way to the back door.

Marie shakes her head. "We're going to have to drag her out of here tonight."

Music starts playing in Xavier's living room that looks more like a ballroom. I notice he has a live band there playing. Marie gets asked to dance by a handsome gentleman in a suit and she shyly agrees. Kate is next, another handsome fellow comes and whisks her away. I peek my head over the crowd, directing my gaze out the back window. Sure enough, Fiona seems to be hitting it off with Xavier's cousin. Xavier clears his throat and I sheepishly turn back face him. He holds his hand out to me, asking me to dance. I place my hand in his shyly and let him lead me to the makeshift dance floor.

Once we're there, he pulls me tight against him and starts to move. My back is against the front of his body as he wraps his arms around my waist. The way he's pressing our bodies together and moving, is nothing short of scandalous. It wasn't like this *last* time we danced. His hands roam over my clothes and he breathes heavily in my ear. Every touch against my skin causes tingles to run through my body. I feel my own breathing becoming heavy as I look forward to each touch. I silently hope he stops this, before I lose control and embarrass us both.

"Did you dress like that to tempt me?" he whispers. "If-so it's working," he breathes.

I'm becoming dizzy and I haven't even had a drink yet. He spins me around to face him and the look in his eyes speaks volumes.

"Ready to have that talk now?" he says, his mouth hanging open slightly. I nod, slowly.

He leads me away from the crowd and up a staircase. We come up to a door and he opens it and steps aside for me to enter. I walk in slowly and hesitantly, feeling unsure of what is about to happen. He follows after me, then walks in front of me to face me. Half of his face is in the dark, and the other half is bathed in the light peeking from the opened door. The intensity radiating from those gold eyes makes me want to look away, but I don't. Xavier gently pushes me back abruptly, my back shutting the door in the process. There's just enough light from outside, to cast a dim glow into the room and onto our faces. He stares straight into my eyes through the dark, as he reaches his arm around me and locks the door.

"No, getting away this time," he flashes me a quick smile, with his perfect white teeth.

I can't tell if he's joking or serious. I laugh a little and he holds my gaze. Oh, he's serious then. He backs away from me slowly and sits on a bed.

"Come here," he commands.

My heart is hammering in my chest now. I walk slowly to the bed, feeling like such a coward. *Where was the wine when I needed it?* Apparently, it made me bold last time. Don't get me wrong, I knew what I was doing, I just had a little help then. Now, I felt *too* aware, too sensitive. Like I did the first time when we were in the jacuzzi at his house on Catalina. Quiet plainly, I was chicken. He watches me closely, not taking his eyes off of me. He opens his legs for me, allowing space for me to stand in between them. I fit between them slowly. He raises his fingertips to the hem of my skirt, dragging them up and down, slowly, all the while keeping his eyes on me.

"What did you want to talk to me about?" I ask, my voice coming out shaky.

His fingertips trace up my arms, causing goosebumps on them. "Why'd you run out on me this morning?" he stares into my eyes. "Did I do something wrong?"

I knew he was going to ask me this but I'm not really sure why I did either, I just sort of...panicked. So I try my best to explain.

"No....I...." I struggle to get the words out. "I have to leave tomorrow night, back to Pennsylvania," I blurt out accidentally, getting straight to the punch.

I had planned on telling him that, just not right away. His mouth drops slightly in surprise. I mentally curse myself and try to backtrack.

"I was just...trying to make things *easier*...you know, for the both of us."

He's silent for a moment, I don't know what he's thinking and waiting for him to answer is painful. His hands drop to mine and he holds them both in his.

"Is that *really* what you want?" he challenges. The question catches me off guard. He searches my eyes.

"I—I don't know," I shake my head. "I don't really have a *choice*..."

"You *always* have a choice," he argues. "What you gave me last night was a *gift*. It was..... the *best* night I've ever had," he smirks up at me. My face is flaming hot and I'm thankful that he can't see it in the dark. I can't believe he said that, my heart stutters from his words. "I'm just going to have to *convince* you to stay," he breathes. He lets go of one of my hands. Then I feel his hand begin to climb underneath my skirt, in between my legs.

Kathey Gray

CHAPTER ELEVEN
White Lies

The next few weeks pass like a blur. I fell fast and I fell hard. The craziest part is that I never saw it coming. I guess I wouldn't know what to look for anyway, since I had never been in love. I've never done drugs before either, but I imagine it feels somewhat like making love with Xavier. Addictive and maddening. Like my last and only lifeline. That's all we seemed to *do* lately. In fact the only time we'd *wear* our clothes is when we would take a break to eat. Sometimes we'd go out to movies or the beach. Or shopping, or to a restaurant. Even then it was hard to keep our hands off of each other.

That night at Xavier's party had ended quickly, despite all of the buildup. Fiona had ended up getting too drunk and vomiting all over the front of Cruz's shirt. Marie beat the door down before me and Xavier could go any further. I told him I had to back home and apologized. The determined look in his eyes told me that somehow things still weren't over. The next evening, Xavier showed up at the airport. He had bought me a dozen roses. He asked me to stay with him for one more day. He promised he'd buy my ticket back when I was ready to leave. I'm still not ready...

My dad has taken over the library since I've been gone. I'm glad he's been so understanding. He told me to take all the time I needed, since my classes don't resume until the fall and it's only July. I know what he wants, he wants me to move on. He'd probably do *anything* for that to happen.

I lie in Xavier's huge bed, feeling completely sated. He's taking a shower before we go out for dinner, when my phone rings. *Shit*, it's Ava. She's back from her honeymoon and must be wondering where I am.

I answer the phone, dreading the questions. "Hey, Ava..." My voice sounds rehearsed.

"Don't you *'hey'* me, honey!" she scolds. I flinch from her acidic tone. "Please tell me that Marie has lost her fucking mind and that you really *aren't* still in California with some stranger you met two weeks ago!"

"Um, well, I *can't* tell you that." I shrink down inside myself.

I hear her gasp into the phone. "I can't believe I *missed* this. Did you *really* give him your V-card?" she asks me, shamelessly.

My face gets hot and I sigh deeply before whispering. "Yes"

"Oh my, I never thought I'd see the day," I hear her smiling into the phone.

"Yeah well, me either," I admit, laughing in disbelief.

"So you're really happy? He's treating you right? When are you coming back?" She bombards me with questions.

I laugh. "Yes and yes and before school starts back up." I pause for a moment. "What about *you!* Tell me all about your honeymoon!" I change the subject. She gushes about how perfect and beautiful everything was and how it'd be a miracle if she weren't pregnant already. "Good for you, I'm so happy for you, Ava."

"You too, Vi—," she says.

"Well I owe it to *you*, really. If it weren't for your inviting Xavier to the wedding, I'd never have went out with him," I remind her, kindly.

"What are you *talking* about Vi?" Ava sounds confused. "I never invited him to the wedding," she confesses.

I feel a chill run through me, suddenly getting an instinctively bad feeling. "What?" I mutter, bemused. And she repeats it.

"I *said* I never invited Xavier to the wedding," she says, sounding more concerned this time.

Just then Xavier walks in and grins at me, towel slung around his waist. I don't know what to say or how to feel. He *lied* to me. So I quickly get off of the phone before I alarm Ava anymore. "Um, I gotta go. I'll text you in a while. I'm so glad you called," I say hurriedly, as Xavier watches me with curiosity.

I hear Ava start to protest. "Vi— wait!" I hear her say.

"Bye Ava!" I say quickly and press end on the call.

Xavier's eyes watch me carefully. "What's up? What did Ava say?" he asks.

I don't know why I use have to use my rehearsed voice when I say. "Oh, nothing. She just wanted to tell me she was back."

He nods. "You're not ready for dinner yet," he observes, looking slightly disappointed.

"Give me twenty minutes," I smile back at him.

I grab my bag and head into the bathroom, away from his observant eyes. I don't know why I feel like

I need a moment alone. I feel betrayed for some reason. Even though, it was really just a small, white lie. It was a lie nonetheless. But was it sweet or creepy that he lied and snuck into the wedding just to see me again? I put on the little black dress that Xavier bought me the other day when we were shopping. I pair it with matching black heels. I curl my hair a little and put on lipstick and mascara. Then I spritz myself with the expensive perfume that Xavier bought me, Chanel No 5. Xavier really is a good guy, he's done nothing but treat me like a princess since the day we met. If he told one little lie just to get me to go out with him, I should probably be flattered. I decide to let it go. Whatever the reason, it probably wasn't enough to cause a concern.

I walk out grinning ear to ear, expecting to find Xavier waiting for me, but he's not in the bedroom. I grab my purse and start to make my way down the staircase. "*Xavier?*" I call, but I don't see him anywhere. I walk into his gigantic living room, still searching. That's when I hear a voice arguing in Spanish. I peer out of the window and see Xavier in the backyard, pacing with his cell phone held up to his ear.

"*Ya te dije, no es problema.*"

I listen, straining to understand.

"*Violeta no sabe.*"

Violeta? Is that my name in Spanish? He's talking about *me!*

"*Si, si, entiendo. Esa no será un problema.*"

I have no idea what he's talking about, but it doesn't sound good. Since when does Xavier even *speak* Spanish? This is the *second* secret I've found about him today. I start to feel nauseous with worry. Surely, I'm overreacting and he just failed to mention it.

"*Déjala fueran de esto, pinche, no me pruebes!*" he growls into the phone, suddenly, causing me to flinch where I stand.

"*Tu mejor,*" he says in a low, threatening voice.

He ends the call and starts heading back inside. Fear of being caught eavesdropping shoots through me and I scramble to find somewhere to hide. I can't run up the stairs fast enough and hiding somewhere else would just make me look suspicious. So I open the front door and pretend to be looking for him out there. He walks in the moment I'm opening the front door.

"Violet," he calls.

I turn with my hand on the handle and act surprised. "*There* you are! I was looking all over for you," I breathe.

He ambles over, his features smooth and seemingly calm. He's good at hiding his emotions, that knowledge makes me feel even more uneasy. "Well I'm right *here*," he pulls me toward him by my waist. "Although I'm not sure I *want* to go out now, seeing you in that dress," he licks his lips, staring into my eyes seductively.

For the first time since our first time, I'm afraid to sleep with him. "But I'm hungry," I whine.

"I am too," he smiles crookedly, lowering his hands to my bottom, digging his fingers into the thin material of my black dress. He starts to inch it upward when I step back.

"You can't have dessert before dinner, didn't your mom teach you?" I scold him playfully.

He makes a low noise in his throat. "Teasing me will just make me want you *more*. Keep it up and you won't be sleeping tonight," he threatens.

I wink at him. "Who said I wanted to *sleep?*" I walk out the front door and he reluctantly follows behind.

I don't know how much longer I can fend off his advances. Xavier's the type of guy who *rises* to a challenge, as opposed to being intimidated by it. But being close to him that way right now will just mess up my head even more. I need to find a way to get away from him for a while. I had the perfect opportunity too. We were going out to dinner in a very public place. All I needed to do was excuse myself to the restroom and not come back.

Simple right?

CHAPTER TWELVE
Dessert And Diamonds

Xavier's eyes smolder at me from across the table. The lighting in the restaurant seems to just amplify the gold in them.

"You're quiet tonight," he observes, watching me too close for comfort.

I flush, not realizing I was being so transparent. "Am I? I must just be tired." I twirl the spaghetti noodles around on my fork. The Italian restaurant Xavier brought me to is impressive. The lighting is dim and romantic. He's been staring at me all night like I'm his dessert. He makes it hard for me to stick to my original plan. But I can't let my lust for him rule over logic. No matter how *hard* that may be.

"I thought you said you weren't planning on sleeping much tonight? I was looking forward to that," he licks his lips. He leans back against the booth seat, resting his head back, gazing at me through hooded eyes. "I can't wait to peel you out of that dress," he whispers, smirking sexily.

I swallow and take a big gulp of my wine to give myself liquid bravery. "I need to use the restroom," I shoot up, knocking the table a little bit. The silverware clinks loudly together and the wine in the glasses sloshes around, almost spilling.

Instead of getting mad, Xavier smirks, entertained. For some reason, he likes it when I'm nervous. It *excites* him, for some inexplicable reason. "Okay, I'll be here," he replies calmly.

I go in search of the restroom. When I find it, I duck into it immediately. I stare at myself in the mirror and take deep breaths. *Is this really happening to me? Am I really dating someone who lies and hides things from me?* It makes me wonder what other things he's deliberately hidden from me. I've been so caught up in him, that I wasn't seeing him clearly. Maybe I don't know him that well after all? It's only been a few weeks, what did I *expect?* That my first would be my last and only? Well, sort of. I guess that's the way a naïve young woman thinks. I can't believe I fell for that. I don't want to *be* that cliché. That "sweep it under the rug" kind of girlfriend. But I can't just walk away, my feelings are too invested in him.

I'll ask him. I owe him that. A chance to come clean and tell me the truth. I'm probably just being emotional and overreacting. I'm sure there are perfectly reasonable explanations for *both* of the things I'm worried about. I take one last deep breath, exit the bathroom and head back to our table. Xavier is waiting for me with a strange glimmer in his eyes. I sit down, refusing to give in to his charms. I'm going to come right out and ask him. I stick my chin out and level my gaze to his. "Xavier I need to ask you something-" I start, but something catches my eye. My pasta is gone and in place of it, is a decadent dessert. I become distracted.

"You ordered me *dessert* already? I wasn't done with my pasta," I complain, feeling like a petulant child.

His face falls a little. "I'm sorry, we can order some to-go if you're still hungry? The dessert here is unbelievable though, I didn't want you to miss out on it."

"Oh...okay," I shake my head, wanting to get back to the matter at hand.

"Try it," he encourages. His eyes twinkle suspiciously.

My lips set into a line. I guess eating dessert won't deter the questions I have lined up for him. I pick up my fork and slice into the decadent cake. Some sort of red glaze pours out of it. I taste it and fall in love immediately. Xavier pokes his fork in and samples it, too. His eyes close in pleasure. I can't look at his face when he does that, it looks an awful like when he—

"What did I tell you? The *best*, right?" he interrupts my wayward thoughts.

I nod. "It's heavenly." I go to take another bite, but my fork hits something hard. "What's *in* this?" I scrunch up my nose. I use my fork to dig out the foreign object. Something glitters inside of the dessert. I must be *dreaming*. I pull the object out with my fork and stare at it from where it rests on the plate. I know what I'm looking at, but my brain doesn't seem to process fully what's happening. Because there's *no* way this can be real. I haven't even known Xavier for a *month*.

There, covered in the deep, red, strawberry glaze, is a diamond ring. It sparkles so bright with its impressive facets, even in the dim light of the restaurant. For some reason the red glaze resembles blood and the glittering diamond amidst it looks disturbing. But I'm pulled from my thoughts by Xavier speaking.

"Violet, I've never felt like this about a woman before. You're so special to me. You're unlike anyone I've known." He reaches his hand across the table and takes mine in his. "I'm in love with your beauty, your innocence, your laugh, your smile, your eyes. I'm in love with *you*. I want you to be mine forever." My eyes drag from the ring up to his face. "I was your first and I want to be your last," he gazes at me from underneath his lashes.

He carefully picks the ring out of the dessert, bringing it to his mouth. He sucks the red glaze off of it, and my eyes are glued to his every move. He slides it on my finger, it fits perfectly. I stare at it in awe, it's easily six carats. It has a thin, white gold band with a giant round diamond in the middle. Simple, but glamorous. He smiles at the ring on my finger.

"Will you do me the honor of being my wife?" he asks, his golden eyes warm.

I'm so awestruck by the turn of events. I thought this was a regular evening of going to out dinner. There was no way I could predict this would ever, in a million years, happen. But then again, it was hard to predict *anything* with Xavier. *What was I going to ask him again? Why* was I worried? I couldn't remember anything. All I could see was the giant sparkling diamond, hypnotizing me with its unspoken promises.

"Violet," Xavier calls my attention back. I look up at him. "Say something," he watches me, a flicker of worry settling onto his usually confident face. I look at the ring, it feels so heavy on my finger. As heavy as the decision I'm about to make. The word is out of my mouth before I can stop it.

"Yes," I whisper.

Xavier's eyes light up. "You *will?*" he smiles triumphantly and reaches across the table and takes my face in his hands. He kisses me hard, the joy radiating off of him. He pulls back. "I can't wait. We should get married right away. We can honeymoon in Greece!" he carries on excitedly. "*Waiter!*" he calls. "Can we get some champagne? This beautiful woman just agreed to *marry* me!"

I sit still, wordless and shell-shocked. I can't believe I just *did* that. I'm *engaged?* The waiter brings over a bottle of champagne in a bucket of ice and two champagne flutes.

"Congratulations!" The waiter smiles at us, his thick mustache twitching when he speaks.

He looks like Super Mario, I think absentmindedly, to myself. Xavier pops the top of the champagne bottle open and pours us each a glass.

He holds his up. "To getting married," he beams. My lips twitch as I lift up my glass to clink it against his.

"To us," I say. I've never seen him this excited before.

This is all happening so *fast*. Everything is like that with Xavier. He always makes me feel like I'm flying or falling, I can't decide which. I hope I'm not making a mistake, I think to myself. He lifts his glass and drinks all the champagne in one drink. I delicately sip mine.

"Well, future Mrs. Daniels, I'm sorry to say, you won't be sleeping a wink tonight. Are you ready to go? I'm ready to make love to my fiancée," he purrs, seductively. His eyes glow with lust. "By the way, what did you want to ask me?" he suddenly remembers.

I feel like I've been sucker punched in the gut. "Nothing, it was nothing," I mumble.

CHAPTER THIRTEEN

Pillow Talk

Well so much for plan "find out what Xavier's hiding", I think, when I wake in the odd hours of the morning. Our naked bodies are entangled together. I raise my chin up to see the evidence all over the room. Empty bottles of champagne are on the bedside table. Our clothes is strewn all over the floor. I really don't know *how* he does it. How he can take *any* situation and seduce its pants off. It's a talent, really. Not that I didn't *enjoy* it, because I did. I enjoyed it *way* too much. But now I'm *engaged?* I lift up my hand to see if it's real and feel the weight of the heavy diamond on my finger. It's a surreal feeling. The sparkling diamond twinkles at me, enchanting me.

Suddenly, a sickening feeling comes over me...*he didn't ask my dad for my hand?* Oh, no. That's bad, *really bad.* My dad is an old-fashioned man and I'm his only daughter. He will definitely expect to approve of anyone I plan on marrying, *before* I marry him! *Duh, Violet!* How could I let something so *important* slip my mind? Xavier was like some sort of sex drug that numbed my mind and clouded it. He made me act stupid. Beyonce's "Drunk In Love" song comes to mind. I know what she means. I start to feel the stress crawling its way up my arms. My head is already pounding from too much champagne. *Great, this is all I need.*

What will Xavier *say?* Will he be *mad? Nervous?* Why didn't he think of this before, if he's serious? What will my dad say? What would he think of Xavier? When will they meet? Will my dad tell him 'no' ? The questions wrack my brain, one after another. When will I meet Xavier's parents? How will I attend college back in Pennsylvania if we're engaged? Does he expect me to transfer or have a long distance relationship? I don't see how that could work out. I realize also, that I barely know about all of Xavier's businesses, he barely talks about work. I wonder why that is? Too stressful? Where has my head been, anyway? I guess it took leave when my body took over. I should ask him about it. As I'm flooding myself with questions, Xavier stirs on top of me.

"*Mmmm,*" he mumbles.

I still and peek to see if he's awake, but his eyes are closed, he must be dreaming.

"*Baby,*" he whispers with his eyes still closed. I crack a smile. *He's having a dirty dream about me?*

All of my worries start to melt away as I listen on with entertainment. I've never heard him 'sleep-talk' before.

"*Trinity*," he mutters.

My body goes stiff as a board. An electric shock runs through me. *Did he just say?* Flashbacks of us talking on the deck about his yacht flash through my mind. The word written on the side of it, like a picture in my brain. *Trinity*, it had read. I search his deceptively innocent features, hoping I heard wrong.

"*Don't go Trinity*," he mutters, before turning the other way and resuming sleeping quietly.

My skin gets that eerie creepy-crawly feeling. I want to crawl out from under him and run away. I want to leave right now. Slide this rock off of my finger and set it on his nightstand and take my bag and go home. That's what any *sane* woman would do, right? Any time a man mutters another woman's name in their sleep, they *should* be toast. But I feel like there has to be some other explanation. There's no way he would lie to me about that, too, *right?*

I want to know the answer, and then I don't. I'm *afraid* to know. *That's* the problem. I don't *want* to believe Xavier is deep down, a bad guy. There is no way I can sleep now. I realize I need to talk to someone about all of this. I need advice and I know just who to ask. I manage to slip out from under Xavier without waking him. I slip on the silk robe

Xavier bought me and grab my cell phone from the nightstand. I tip toe quietly through the large house. I still think it's too much house for one person. Even too much for *two*. I get down the stairs successfully undetected and unlock the back door, slipping through it.

Once I'm outside, the cool breeze gives me goosebumps. I hug the thin fabric of the robe tighter around me. I slide my phone over and search my contacts. I press call and stare at the reflection of the moonlight on Xavier's swimming pool. The phone rings five times before someone answers.

"*Hello?*" a sleepy voice mumbles.

"Ava?" I ask, as if I already don't know it's her.

"*Vi— is everything okay?*" she sounds concerned. "*It's three in the morning,*" she adds.

I sigh. "I know, I'm *sorry*. Yeah, I'm fine. It's just, I really needed someone to talk to," I breathe nervously, fiddling with my robe string. "I'm sorry I woke you up," I add.

"*It's okay,*" she laughs, sleepily. "*You're my best friend, you can do that.*"

I laugh. "So you'll talk to me right now? Sure you won't fall asleep?" I ask, wondering.

"*I'll try my best not to, shoot.*" I can imagine her smirking through the phone.

I don't mean to spill my guts, but that's exactly what I end up doing. I tell her almost every detail of mine and Xavier's relationship, up to our surprise engagement. I leave out the part about him muttering another woman's name, for some reason I feel like it's too personal to talk about now. The wound is still too raw.

"Are you still there?" I ask Ava, when I don't hear her respond immediately.

"*Yes, yes, of course I am,*" she breathes, sounding overwhelmed. She sighs, "*I don't know, Vi— your relationship is moving so fast. I mean, you're engaged now?*" she asks, her voice incredulous.

"You think we're rushing into it?" I ask, feeling somewhat relieved that I'm not the only one who feels like I'm riding a roller coaster at full speed. Sure, it's thrilling and adrenaline pumping. But with all of the unexpected twists, loops and turns, it's becoming too much to handle.

"*Yes,*" she says. "*And, well, the fact that he's not been completely honest with you isn't a good sign either. The things he lies about, they're...not really the average 'guy lies'. He just seems suspicious. I don't know... I kind of have a weird feeling about him. You need to be careful,*" she warns. The fact that my best friend is worried about it, makes me even more uncomfortable. Maybe my instincts *were* trying to tell me something?

Suddenly, I feel like someone is watching me. Paranoid, I turn and look over my shoulder, up at Xavier's bedroom window that overlooks the backyard. When I don't see him staring down at me, I take a deep breath. "I don't know what to do, I'm...I'm in love with him," I confess.

"*Well I would hope you're in love with someone you just agreed to marry!*" she scoffs. "*But are you sure it's love or is it lust?*" Ava asks, in a speculative tone.

"What?" I ask, caught off guard.

"*Love is forever, someone you would die for. Someone you don't ever want to live without. Lust is infatuation, addiction, someone you can't keep your hands off of. Now are you in love or lust with Xavier?*"

I grow quiet, thoughtful. What I have with Xavier can't possibly just be lust, *can it?*

Ava grows impatient for my answer and breaks the tense moment. "*Oh, Vi— what are we going to do with you?*" she giggles. "*Your first relationship,*" she croons with motherly admiration.

I feel so embarrassed to be this inexperienced, when Ava already has it all figured out. "Shut up!" I laugh, my cheeks burning hot.

She cackles.*"You'll figure it out. But first, if you seriously are considering marriage, which I don't think you're quite ready for that, but that's just my opinion. You need to follow your heart and you need to find out the truth. You need to ask Xavier about the things that are bothering you. If he comes clean and you're satisfied with his answers, then you probably have nothing to worry about."*

"And if I'm not?" I ask, nervously chewing my nail.

"That's up to you. But if it were me, I'd chalk it up to one outrageous summer fling and come back home before things get messy."

I sigh.

"*Wait*," Ava remembers, suddenly.

"What?" I ask, my attention piqued.

"*Did he ask your dad first? To marry you?*"

I sigh deeply. "*No*," I whine.

"*Uh-oh*," she says.

"Yeah," I breathe.

I thank Ava for talking to me at such a ridiculous time in the morning and for being the best friend ever and end the call. She's given some things to think about, even more than I had before. But she's also given me some clarity, the kind only your best friend can. I slip back through the door, closing it quietly. I turn back around, about to head back upstairs when I nearly go into cardiac arrest. Xavier is standing in front of me, a few feet away, wearing low-slung pajama pants and no shirt. His eyes are narrowed, his expression guarded.

"What were you doing outside?" his deep voice startles me. He sounds suspicious, maybe even a bit angry.

CHAPTER FOURTEEN

Avoidance

For a second I'm frozen stiff, caught red-handed. But then my instincts kick in.

"I—I was just getting some fresh air, I wasn't feeling good."

Xavier walks slowly over to me, measuring me with his eyes. I don't know why I feel so nervous. So afraid to admit what I was really doing. Even though talking to my best friend on the phone is hardly a *crime*. Even if we were talking about *him*. He stands above me, his golden eyes penetrating.

"Oh, I'm sorry to hear that. Do you think it was the *dinner?*" he asks in a menacingly soft voice.

I feel a chill run through me. "I'm not sure, but I think the air helped," I laugh, uncomfortable.

"That's good," he says running his hands up and down my arms. "You're cold," he says.

"That's why I came in," I inform him.

"It's funny..." he starts.

I look up. "What is?"

"When I came down the stairs, I could *swear* I heard you talking to someone...on the phone," he gazes into my eyes, scrutinizing.

I swallow the dry lump in my throat, wishing for a way to wiggle out of his threatening stare. "Really? That's weird. Maybe you heard the TV?" I suggest.

I see suspicion flash in his eyes, but he smiles anyway. "Yeah, you're probably right. Come on, let's get you back upstairs, so I can warm you back up," he winks.

       I had to convince Xavier that I was sick last night just to keep his hands off of me. I decided it would be best to ask him all of my tough questions in the morning. I'd had my fill of drama for the evening. We're in the kitchen and he's cooking for me, shirtless. As if I needed *another* distraction. He fries some potatoes with onions and bell peppers. The smell coming from the pan is delightful. I realize how ironic this situation is, him looking like the perfect fiancé at the moment and all. It almost makes me forget about all the suspicions I have about him. Almost.

I clear my throat. "Xavier, I need to talk to you about some things...that are important," I say, bravely.

He looks up at me, his hair falling into his eyes. "Okay," he smiles, waiting.

"Well, I actually wanted to ask you, I mean..." I stall, fighting the urge to chicken out. Being under Xavier's golden gaze isn't child's play.

He raises his eyebrows at me. "Yes?" He picks up the wooden spoon and tastes the potatoes. I want to yell, '*stop doing that! I'm trying to think!*' But I refrain.

I sigh. *I need to get this over with.* I'm *engaged* to this man for Christ's sake!

"Ava said she never invited you to her wedding," I spit out, cringing at the words as the leave my lips.

Xavier doesn't flinch. He doesn't *blink*. He just stares at me for a moment and I don't know what it means. Then he cracks a smile and starts laughing. I'm confused by his reaction. When he finally stops, I just look at him, unsure of what to think. He comes around the kitchen island and stands in front of me.

He lifts my chin up with his fingers, holding it, delicately.

"She told me not to *tell* you," he explains. "She must've not wanted to *embarrass* you."

"She *did?*" I ask, highly skeptical. That doesn't *sound* like Ava at all. She was never 'afraid' to embarrass me, in fact she *loved* to.

"Yes," he smiles at me, staring straight into my eyes.

He's lying. He's looking straight into my eyes and *lying!* Maybe *he's* just embarrassed? He's too worried to ruin his 'playboy' status and admit the lengths he went to to go out with me? If so, I sort of feel sorry for him...and it's kind of cute. Maybe I should let that one go and get to the more important ones? It hardly seems as significant as the other things I wanted to ask him. Well, I'm glad I started with the easiest one. He leans down and kisses me briefly on this lips, before resuming his spot in front of the stove. He turns it off and announces, "breakfast!"

We sit down outside on his back patio eating the delicious potato and egg scramble. There are hints of spice in the food, it reminds me of the second question I want to ask him.

"Can I ask you another question?" I hedge.

"Sure," he smiles, but his eyes are tight.

"Are you....latino?" I ask, feeling so awkward. I hope I didn't offend him.

His eyes look vacant when he answers me. "My mother is Italian," he says.

"...Oh.." *Italian?* I guess Italian and Spanish *sound* a lot alike.

"What made you ask?" he says, keeping his eyes downward, on his food. I detect the slight irritation of his tone.

"Oh, well, just...because of all the spicy food you like," I answer.

That's partly true. I don't know why I feel so nervous asking him these questions. He's the one who should be shrinking down in guilt. But somehow he has me feeling like *I'm* the villain.

"Do you *speak* Italian?" I challenge.

"Si, amore mio," he smirks.

Well, shit. Maybe he really *is* Italian? My jaw drops. "What did you say?"

"I said, 'yes, my love'," he smirks.

"Oh....why didn't you ever mention that you spoke another language *before?*" I ask, in awe.

He shrugs, nonchalantly. "Never came up. I traveled a lot when I was younger, so I speak a few languages."

A few? How has he never said this to me? I don't know if I should be turned on or upset. He's so...mysterious. That's when I realized, I'm engaged to a stranger.

"Well, that's really...cool," I say, lamely. Too occupied in my own head to respond appropriately.

"Is it 'cool'?" he teases. I nod. "Is that all you wanted to ask me?" he inquires.

I still needed to ask him about his work and then there's that other small thing...the one that I'm most afraid to hear the answer to. I decide to start again with the easier one.

"Yes. Now that we're engaged, I thought I should know more about your work," I inform him, matter-of-factly.

"Oh, really?" he snickers. "What do you want to know?"

We're both finished eating and are seated across from each other, lost in conversation.

"Well, for starters, how many businesses do you own and where are they?" I ask, unashamed of my nosiness this time.

He seems unfazed by my prying. "I own a few night clubs in California and Miami. I also have my own online custom suit company, we ship internationally," he says simply.

"*Suits?*" I ask, in disbelief.

"Suits," he nods. "I believe a man should be impeccably dressed when he does business."

"Do you *design* them?"

"Of course," he beams. He rises. "Are you done?"

"With the questions or my food?" I wonder aloud.

"Both," he grins.

"Yes to the food, not yet with the questions," I admit.

He laughs. "Well, speaking of work, I need to get ready to go into the club for a while. Can we finish this later?" he asks.

I pause, surprised. He hasn't been to work in the last two weeks. "Of course," I reply, out of politeness. Even though all he's done is plant the seed to a tree of questions in my brain.

"Great," he winks.

I stay seated out on the back patio, staring at the pool water, trying to take inventory of his answers so far. They do seem legitimate. He walks back outside already fully dressed and looking suave.

"That was fast," I comment.

"Why are you still out here?" he asks.

"I was thinking about taking a dip in the pool," I smile up at him.

"Sounds relaxing. I'll see you in a few hours," he says.

"Okay," I smile sweetly.

That should be enough time to search through some of his things. I need to find out who this 'Trinity' is.

He leans down and pecks me on the cheek. "Don't have too much fun without me," he winks.

"I'll try my best," I tease.

I watch him walk away. I'm going to ask him the last question tonight. I'm going to ask him, 'who is Trinity?' I just hope he finally comes clean. If he doesn't, I might have to call off the engagement.

Kathey Gray

CHAPTER FIFTEEN
The Ugly Truth

Nothing. I got nothing.

I searched his place up and down and found nothing. It's like this isn't even his *real* place. I couldn't even find anything that would be considered a personal attachment. Maybe he was renting this place temporarily as a summer house? I float in Xavier's pool on my back, staring at the fading blue sky. It's almost evening now and he still isn't back. It's the longest he's left me alone before. It's given me time to myself to think clearly. It's also given me time to be alone and miss home.

I let myself sink to the bottom of the pool and just sit there until I run out of breath and have to come back up for air. Then I swim quickly to the other side. The smell of the chlorine invades my senses. I can even smell the lining of the pool, it must be new. Any other girl would be in heaven right now. Sun shining on a perfect California day, swimming in her rich fiancé's pool. But I just miss the crisp air of Pennsylvania. The smell of all the dusty, old books in the library. My dad and Ava...

Suddenly, I hear voices, speaking in Spanish or Italian...or maybe it *was* Spanish? I duck my head down in alarm, peeking over the edge of the pool. Xavier never said anything about having visitors over, did he? I can see two dark figures moving around inside of the house. *What the hell do they think they're doing?* How did they even get *in?* I start to get angry. What makes them think that they can go through his *house?* I start to get out of the pool, ready to have a word with them, until I hear a loud bang. I flinch and sink quickly back down into the water. I resume peeking from the side of the pool. They start throwing stuff around, loudly and carelessly. Every time I hear a thud or a loud crash, my heart jumps inside of my chest. *They're completely trashing the place!*

They argue with each other in Spanish, I'm sure of it, as I watch helplessly from where I stand. I can't do anything or get out without being caught. Being caught, I'd assume would be the worst thing for me right now. Especially in my clothes-less state. My bikini doesn't exactly leave much to the imagination after all. Who the hell *are* these guys? *Robbers?* There's *no* way that Xavier *knows* them, right? I feel nauseous suddenly. *This is what you get for promising to marry a stranger!* My subconscious screams at me. Just then, my cell phone rings.

My head snaps to it, it's sitting on the table by the back door. *Please don't hear it. Please don't hear it.* I silently beg. *Stop calling me! Whoever is calling!* What if it's Xavier? What if he was trying to *warn* me? But one of the figures in the house turns and walks toward the back door, peeking out of its windows. I see his face for a split second before I duck my head out of sight. My chin is resting on the water now and my view is blocked. That split second is *all* I needed, to know that these guys are *not* the kind of guys that *anyone* would want to mess with. The guy I saw had a huge, vertical scar running from underneath his eye, all the way down to the curve of his jaw. I stand stock still in the water, straining to listening over the sound of my heart pounding hard and loud in my chest. The phone stops ringing finally, but the damage has already been done. I listen as the back door opens. I can hear both of the men outside now, they sound like they're inspecting my phone. My heartbeat picks up pace. I left my dress on the chair. *Shit!* I hear as they notice someone is still here. Even though every word is in Spanish, I can tell by their voices, *they know*.

It's quiet for a moment and I begin to wonder if they went to look for me inside. I poke my head up, thinking it might be safe, of course I'm wrong. Both of the men, who were still standing in the same spot, looking at my phone, notice me and look up. They have guns, I realize in horror... *big* ones.

They point at me. "*Alli está!*"

Great, I'm going to die. They're either going to shoot me now or catch me and kill me later. Well, I'd like to prolong my death for as long as possible. So with adrenaline running high, I surprise myself by hopping out of the pool swiftly, splashing water everywhere. I run as fast as I can, towards the back gate. I hear gunshots loud and sharp coming from behind me, piercing my ear drums. I hear the strange *whooshing* sound they make when the bullets hit the water. I don't even know if I've been shot, I refuse to turn around or stop. I'm running so hard, too numb to feel anything even if I *had* been shot. Tears start to burn in my eyes, as I expect the worst. I could drop dead at any moment.

My hands hit the gate and I frantically fumble with the handle. A panicked shriek escapes my lips. I'm not going to be fast enough, they're going to kill me. I hear four more gun shots and scream at the top of my lungs as a last, pathetic defense. Somehow, I'm still alive. I finally get the handle open, when I feel hands grab me from behind. My whole body stiffens in terror as I scream again. A large hand covers my mouth to muffle the sound. I kick and struggle with my captor. I watch helplessly, as he holds me with one hand with ease for a moment, using the other to shut the gate. *No!* My chances for escaping this are almost non-existent now. My captor pins me against the brick wall of the side of the house, trapping me between the wall and him. Then he turns me around to face him. I prepare for the worst, a gun pointed directly at me, the guy with the scary, scar face, a knife to my throat, being assaulted. I prepared for almost anything but this....

My captor lets go of my mouth. "*Xavier?*" I whisper, in disbelief.

Xavier is still wearing the same clothes he was when he left to work today. He looks unfazed and perfect as usual, except for one thing. A deadly looking, black gun hangs from his left hand. "Hey, baby. Sorry I'm late," he drawls.

"Xavier, what the *hell?* What...what's going on? Where..." I look past him, into the backyard. "There were some men here," I say finally, breathless and confused.

"Yes, I know. I'm sorry they scared you. Don't worry, you're safe now." He drops the gun and holds me by the arms.

When he lets go of me, I look him square in the eye. "Xavier, why do you have that gun? Where are the men?"

"I took care of them, don't worry about it. We have to get you out of here, we have to go somewhere safe," he says, emphatically.

"But—"

Before I can finish, Xavier has picked up the gun again, and is already pulling me by the hand, towards the yard. "C'mon, we have to move quickly," he rushes me.

As he's dragging me along, I see the two men lying on the ground by the pool. They're not moving, then I notice the blood. I gasp and my knees fall out from under me. They're *dead*. Xavier catches me and holds me up with his arm.

"They're....."

Words fail me and I can't even finish the sentence. But he does for me.

"Yes, they're dead," he says, gravely.

He drags me past them, holding me in one arm and the giant gun in his other hand. He opens the back door and signals for me to go in. I pause, looking back at the bodies.

"You...*killed* them....?" I ask, even though I know he did.

"I *had* to, to protect you," he explains, his eyes serious.

"Who *are* they?" I demand.

"We can talk about that later, we need to hurry up and get out of here. More will be coming soon."

That gets my legs moving. Then I remember my phone, I turn back around to get it and my dress off of the table outside. Then we go back inside of the house. I slip my dress over my head and stare at Xavier, not knowing what to do next.

"Upstairs," he commands. *Why is he still carrying that gigantic gun?*

I run up the stairs, with him following close behind me. We get to his bedroom. "Get some shoes on and pack your things, we're going to have to go away for a while."

CHAPTER SIXTEEN
Flight

After Xavier pretty much dragged me out of the house and into his car, we were on our way to the airport. "Are you going to tell me where we're going, now?" I huff, still rattled from everything from happened. I'm hoping he's going to say that we're going to fly back to Pennsylvania, my home, where I'll be safe.

Xavier smiles over at me, looking the epitome of calm. "On our honeymoon," he winks.

My mouth drops. *"Honeymoon?* We haven't even gotten *married* yet, Xavier! What are you *talking* about?" His mouth sets into a flat line and he looks away, disappointed. He's disappointed with *me?*

Alarm bells are going off like crazy in my head. *This isn't right. None* of this is right. My pulse is racing so fast, adrenaline surges through me. I need to get away from him, *now*. I need to get back home.

I have the urge to take my cell phone out and type an alarm message to my friends and family. But under the ever observant view of Xavier, I know that I wouldn't be able to. I try another tactic.

"Xavier, I would really like to go back to Pennsylvania. We'd be perfectly safe there and then you can ask my dad for my hand, properly?" I offer.

He keeps his eyes on the road. "We're not going to Pennsylvania," he shakes his head. "We're going to Greece, we're going on our honeymoon," he says, decidedly.

My heart drops. I can't *believe* him. Is he really trying to tell me that I can't go *home?* He doesn't own me! And I'm not his wife yet! My hands are shaking slightly, but I have to know. I have to ask him about the men. I have to know just *who* exactly I got myself engaged to.

"Xavier...who were those men? Why did they try to kill me?" I ask, shakily.

He sighs heavily. "They were people from my past. They only tried to kill you to get to me."

"Your *past?*" I raise my brows at him.

He looks at me. "Yes, my past. Everyone has one, *right*? Mine just happens to be a little.. complicated."

"Complicated, *how?*" I ask, feeling like I want to jump out of his car while it's still driving.

He's growing more and more irritated by the moment, I know I'm about to run out of time to question him.

"Well," he says, with his jaw strained. "I used to have a price on my head. That was before I got out and changed my life. Before I met *you*," he smiles at me, fondly. He reaches one hand over to caress my cheek. I want to cringe away, but I maintain the contact.

"How *long* before?" I gulp. The words 'price on my head' are ringing over and over again in my ears.

He turns back to the road again, all business. "I've been out for a few years now. I haven't had any problems in a long time. I don't know how they found me this time. Maybe I got a little too comfortable in my business decisions. Either way, they know about *you* now," he looks over at me, worriedly. "But don't worry, I'll keep you safe. As long as you stay with me, you'll be safe."

I beg to differ. The last thing I feel right now is *safe*. I want to be as far away from him as possible. He has it all wrong, as long as I'm by his side, I'm in *danger*.

"Xavier," I say, carefully. "You said those men were from your past. What exactly did you *do* in your past?" I hedge.

There's a long pause of silence in the car as he decides whether or not he wants to tell me. He finally relents.

He says in a low, measured voice, "I operated a drug cartel."

Shit. Shit, shit, shit!!!

"But like I said, I've *changed*," he says, emphatically. "I'm not the guy I used to be," he laughs. How can he be *laughing* right now? He notices my expression and adds, "we'll be safe in Greece."

Something strikes me then, a moment of realization. "I don't have a passport, Xavier," I inform him. "I can't go to Greece."

He smiles at me, shrugging a little. "I've already had one made for you," he admits.

My face scrunches up in disbelief. "*How?*"

"I may be out of the game, but that doesn't mean that I forgot how to play," he turns his face back to the road, smiling smugly.

We arrive to the airport moments later. Xavier parks his car and gets our bags. He looks around before grabbing my hand and pulling me along. I follow along, scanning the parking lot with my eyes, being scared to death that someone might be looking for us. I feel so helpless. Xavier buys us tickets as I try to come up with ways to get away from him in my mind. We make it through security somehow, even though I was hanging on to blind hope that Xavier would get caught with a weapon and be detained. He's too smart for that. We sit, waiting by our gate.

"Are you hungry?" he offers.

I feel too sick to eat anything. "No," I answer him.

"I'm starved. Come, walk with me. I'll buy you a magazine or something for the flight. It's going to be a long one," he informs me.

I get up and walk with him, over to a little airport café. "How long?"

"Eighteen hours," he smiles. "And we'll be stopping, twice."

My body already feels defeated. I feel like I can't last another eighteen *minutes* with this man, how can I possibly last eighteen *hours?* We get to the café and Xavier orders us a sandwich and smoothie. I notice a bathroom next door to the café and an idea forms. "I need to use the restroom," I say. Xavier is distracted, talking to the woman about his sandwich, he glances down at me and nods. He lets go of my hand, turning back to the woman. I walk away nervously and open the door to the restroom. I turn to see if Xavier is looking, but he's reading a magazine. I let go of the door and walk away, turning a corner, removing myself from his line of sight. I start walking briskly away, glancing behind me the whole time to see if Xavier is coming. I turn another corner and start jogging. I see the escalator that goes down to the first floor. I can see the doors that exit to outside from here. My heart is thumping loudly in my chest. I pull out my phone and press Ava's name. The escalator carries me closer and closer to my freedom as my phone rings. I grow impatient and start to push through the people, trying to get there faster. I turn around one last time to check for Xavier, happy to not find him.

Ava answers, finally when I turn back around. "*Hello?*"

I smack hard into somebody at that exact moment. I look up to see Xavier staring down at me, anger flashes in his eyes but he smiles anyway.

"There you are my little dove, did you get lost?"

I hang up on Ava quickly, before he figures out who I was calling. "I...yeah...I..." I have no idea what to say.

He *knows*. He was waiting for me at the bottom of the escalator.

"Let's get you back to where you belong," he says, putting his hand on my shoulder, urging me forward a little too roughly.

CHAPTER SEVENTEEN
Turbulence

The flight is ridiculously long, but seems even longer
with every awkward second of silence that I have to
endure sitting next to Xavier the whole time. He
keeps a watchful eye on me, holding onto my hand
for the remainder of the flight. I grow annoyed every
time a flight attendant passes by, smiling a little too
politely at Xavier. Their gazes lingering on his face to
the point of it almost being rude to me, if we were a
normal couple in love, that is. Their gaze would
reluctantly slide to mine in disappointment,
probably thinking 'lucky girl'. Except they don't
know that I'm basically being held against my free
will. If it were up to me, I'd be safe at home with my
dad right now. Not on a plane to mine and Xavier's
imaginary honeymoon. Xavier, my fiancé, that I
barely know. Xavier, ex-head drug cartel operator.
Xavier, not actually Italian, but some sort of Latin
descent, like I'd guessed initially. Xavier, who once
loved someone named Trinity, who he also named
his boat after. *Where was she now?* Would he tell

me the truth now that everything was being put on the table? Something in my gut tells me that now's not the time to ask him. It's almost time to land and my bladder was starting to hurt. Xavier hadn't let me move an inch since I failed at my little escape plan. He also took away my phone.

"Xavier, I have to go to the bathroom," I glance at him.

He smiles at me like he knows better. "I'm not playing that game with you again, Violet," his narrowed eyes glitter at me.

"I'm not playing a *game*, I have to *go*. Since I never did....the, um, first time," I add, meekly.

I watch the irritation flash through his eyes again and get nervous. A resentful grin spreads across his face as he chuckles darkly, bitterly shaking his head. He leans in close to me, like he's going to kiss me, my throat dries up. He wraps his free arm around my neck, pulling me down like he's going to whisper something in my ear. But his hand stops underneath the nape of my neck and he grabs a fistful of my hair. He holds it tight within his grasp, making my eyes water. His lips press against my ear.

"Don't make me lose my temper, mi amor," he threatens. "I don't think you'd *like* it very much," he adds. His breath against my ear, along with his threat, causes chills to run down my spine. "Now, make it *fast*," he growls, releasing me.

I sit up, alarmed, looking to see if anyone else saw. But no one else seems to notice anything amiss. His eyes speak volumes as he takes me by the hand, leading me to where the bathrooms are. I follow along, tripping over my own feet. I feel more afraid of him than ever before. How are people not *noticing* the frightened look in my eyes? I feel like reaching out and grabbing one of them by the collar of their shirts and screaming 'help me!' But I don't, I just keep walking forward like the coward I am. When we reach the bathrooms, Xavier ushers me into one. He even closes the door for me, then has the audacity to press his back against the door to wait for me. I sigh and shake my head. Well if he wants to hear me *pee*, then I guess, so be it. As I sit down, I hear a flight attendant asking Xavier to sit back down in his seat, my ears perk up.

"I'm waiting for my wife," he explains. *Wife?!!*

"Well, can you wait over by your *seats?*" she asks him, annoyed.

I wait, wondering if this woman is a God-send and is going to get him off of my back for a change. But of course, he always has smooth words lined up.

"She's sick and she asked me to wait outside. *Pregnant*," he whispers the last part.

I stiffen from where I sit. *Pregnant?! We're already married and now I'm pregnant?!?* The lies just pour out of Xavier's mouth like chocolate syrup onto ice cream, smooth and sweet.

"Oh, well...that's so *sweet* of you," I hear the ice in her voice melt. "Do you two need anything else?" she offers.

The way her voice wavers and then changes makes me sick. He made *her* feel guilty about following protocol. He really is a smooth criminal.

"No, I think we're fine for now," he whispers. "'Thank you," he adds.

I can just imagine the sweet smile he must've offered her, the way his eyes twinkled. I know, because I fell for it, too.

I finish in the bathroom, but don't flush the toilet immediately. I search the small bathroom for some sort of escape or answer to get me away from Xavier. He must instinctively know what I'm trying to do, because he taps on the door. "Violet, baby, are you doing okay?" he asks in a deceptively soft voice. The sound makes me flinch.

Baby! Hmmph! He keeps making me more and more angry.

"Fine," I call back, working to sound sweet.

The pilot announces that we're about to land.

"Good, well hurry up, we're about to land." He tries to mask his irritation with me.

"Sir, you're going to have to take your seat now. We're landing." I hear a male's voice say. Thank goodness, a *man!* Someone Xavier *can't* charm! Unless...unless he's *gay?*

Please don't be gay!

"My pregnant wife is sick in there, I have to wait for her," Xavier uses the same line on him.

"I understand sir, but I'm going to need you take your seat. I will assist your wife back to her seat," the man reassures him.

A smile starts to creep onto my face. What will he say to *that?*

"But she's *sick*, I need to be with her," he stands firm.

"I *understand* that sir. She will be assisted," the man repeats, in a calm voice.

I sense a struggle coming....

Xavier must be wavering because it's silent a moment.

"Am I going to have to get security to escort you to your seat?" The man threatens.

Silence again. My jaw starts to drop. Will he make them get security? That certainly would be good for *me*, then I could leave on my own free will. *Yes, please!* I think. *Get security!* Could I *be* so lucky? But at the end of the silence I hear the male flight attendant say, "thank you, sir."

Damn it, he complied. But he's going to sit down, without me....

"Ma'am how are you doing in there? Are you alright? I'm going to have to ask you to wrap it up, if at all possible. We are about to land," I hear the flight attendant say.

"I'm fine, I'm coming out," I inform him.

I unlock the door and slide out, looking out for Xavier. But before I can whisper to the flight attendant that I need help, Xavier has already returned, having sat in a nearby empty seat that wasn't his.

"*Sir*....." the man starts again. But Xavier ignores him.

"Are you okay, honey? I was so *worried*," he enthuses. Man, this guy can *act*. His eyes are so damn *convincing*. He takes my hand and quickly escorts me away. As soon as our backs are turned, he squeezes my fingers, crushing them in his hand.

"Why can't you behave like a *good* little girl?" he whispers, his voice menacingly quiet.

I whimper quietly and bite my lip to hide the pain. When we get to our row of seats he has me sit in his seat by the window, so he can box me in. "No more bathroom breaks," he says, finally. I flex my fingers and feel the soreness already starting.

We arrive in Denver by 9 p.m. and pretty much have to run for our gate. We get on the plane, heading to Frankfurt, France. I can't believe I'm even *going* to France, it makes me wish the circumstances were different so I could actually *enjoy* it. We eat on the plane, before I fall asleep. The flight is almost ten hours long and I'm beyond exhausted at this point. When we get to France it's already one p.m. It's cloudy and looks much cooler outside than I guessed it would be. Unfortunately, we have a two hour layover and no view of the Eiffel Tower. Xavier eventually has to let me use the bathroom again, but stands outside of the door to wait for me. Then we get on a plane to Athens and that flight is almost three hours long with a three hour layover. I'm starting to get dizzy from all the traveling and time zone changes. Finally, we get on a plane to Santorini, it's eleven p.m. It's a forty-five minute flight, thank goodness, the shortest flight so far. It's almost midnight by the time we arrive. Xavier arranged for a car to pick us up. The colorful lights of the city sparkle even in the midnight hour. The ocean glitters onyx in the night. I have to keep my jaw from dropping. Xavier's watching me, enjoying my reaction. I don't want to give him the satisfaction of looking amazed.

"Is it everything you hoped for, mi amor?" he asks.

But out of fear of my life at the moment, I have to play nice. I hate the fact that I'm actually being honest when I say, "it's more than I hoped for."

CHAPTER EIGHTEEN
Santorini Princess

We step out of the taxi and arrive at a chic, white hotel. *Santorini Princess* the sign reads. Despite our midnight arrival, the bellboys run to our aid immediately, greeting us and collecting our bags, professional as always. Xavier checks us in as my eyes take in the decadence of this hotel. The floors are all marble, the furnishings are white and pristine and the walls and curtains are all in varying shades of cream. This place oozed luxury. For a moment, I forget that my life is in danger, and then Xavier grabs my hand.

"Pretty swanky, isn't it?" he murmurs in my ear.

I fight the urge to flinch away from him.

"I would've rather went to my house, but it's a little more off the beaten path, if you know what I mean. This was much closer and I know you're as tired as I am," he shrugs. "Don't worry, we'll only stay here a night or two. I have a lot to show you and we'll have plenty of time to christen our house later," he smiles.

"Mr. and Mrs. Daniels? Your room is ready, follow me this way."

Mrs. Daniels!!! My mouth drops open and my eyes widen. He's really pretending we're already *married!*

The concierge turns on his heel before he can see my shocked expression.

Xavier smiles at me. "After you, Mrs. Daniels." He urges me forward by pushing me by the small of my back.

I follow reluctantly, wondering if I should attempt to tip off the concierge about Xavier. The last time I tried that, it didn't go so well. Either did the last time I tried to get away. We pass corridor after corridor and window after window, overlooking the gigantic, black sea. The bell boys follow after with our luggage, which is only two bags. The concierge stops at room number forty-three. He hands Xavier the keys.

"Here you are. My name is Giorgios if you need anything, just dial the front desk and ask for me. Complementary champagne and strawberries will be sent shortly, for the happy couple," the tan, spritely little man smiles at us.

"Thank you, Giorgios." Xavier nods at him.

I try to meet Giorgios' eyes to send him some kind of signal, but he just bows and rushes off, leaving me with Xavier and the bell boys. Xavier slides the key in and opens the door, revealing a magnificent room. The decor matches that of the hotel lobby, sleek furniture and cream and white colored fabrics adorn the bed, curtains and furniture. Sitting atop one of the white bedside tables, beside the lamp, is a giant crystal vase containing a dozen white roses. The sheer white curtains flow with the breeze coming from the open balcony doors. The ocean and moonlight shine in the distance, luring even the most patronizing of guests in with its seductive glow. The bell boys set down our bags and Xavier slips them each a generous tip in their palms. They leave quickly thanking him and wishing us a pleasant evening. *My* evening is going to be *anything* but pleasant. To others, we look like a happy, newly-wed couple. No one would guess that Xavier, handsome and charming as he is, is holding me against my will and has gotten us into a mighty mess with his past occupation as a drug lord. He took my cell phone, and now I'm all the way in Santorini, Greece. He's turned my biggest fantasy into a nightmare. I stand, growing more fearful by the second, in the center of the room. I don't know where to sit, I don't know what to *do* or how to *act*. Xavier's made it clear that being *myself* is unacceptable, pretending was the only option I *had*.

"Sit down, dear. Relax..." Xavier walks by me, his hand grazing across my shoulders.

I watch him as he passes me and walks around the room, casually, getting comfortable. Slowly, I walk over to the breakfast nook in the corner of the room. Xavier clears his throat and I look over at him.

He's staring at me. "Not there," he says. *"There,"* he points at the bed. "On the bed," his eyes twinkle darkly at me. A small, satisfied smile touches his lips.

I gulp, hesitating. I don't *want* to get in the bed with him. I don't even want to be in the same *room* with him. The man who used to set my heart a flutter, has started to *scare* me to death. *How can I go to bed with him? Can I act that well? Will he try to hurt me now?* I don't trust him at all.

"*Mrs. Daniels,*" he says in a playful, scolding tone. He shakes his head slowly, while walking over to me. My heart pumps slow and hard in my chest. I'm readying myself for anything at this point. I turn around completely to face him. He looks down at me, his golden eyes glowing. "Tonight is our honeymoon," he purrs. "You might as well get *used* to being in the bed," he says in a velvety voice. A shudder runs through me as his hands land on my waist and squeeze. There's a knock on the door and my heart leaps in my throat.

"Ah, room service," Xavier smiles.

I let out the breath I didn't know I was holding. My heart races in desperation. I couldn't be *more* relieved to be interrupted. Xavier walks over to the door and opens it. The concierge that showed us to our room earlier, Giorgios, is back.

"Complementary champagne and strawberries!" he announces, flamboyantly, wheeling a cart in. The cart contains a silver covered dish and a bucket of ice with a champagne bottle sticking out.

"Wonderful," Xavier smiles.

Giorgios lifts the champagne out of the bucket of ice and pops the cork, pouring it into a chute for me first and then Xavier. He hands us the glasses. "To your dream honeymoon in Santorini!" he cheers, nodding his dark head at us.

"I'll drink to that," Xavier clinks his glass against mine.

I try to smile, but I know it doesn't seem convincing.

"Is there anything else I can help you with tonight?" Giorgios asks us both.

"No that'll be all for—"

"Yes."

Xavier and Giorgios' heads both snap to me. Xavier is already shooting me warning glances.

"*Yes?* Mrs. Daniels? What can Giorgios help you with, my Dahlia?"

I blush from Giorgios' nickname. *Did he just call me a flower?*

"I'm...I'm famished from the trip. Do you have a menu?"

Giorgios' brown eyes light up. "Yes, of course! I will send one right up!"

"Thank you," I smile gratefully at him.

"Of course. I will be right back with a menu!" he rushes off.

The door closes and Xavier covers his mouth with his hand. He leans against it. "I *know* what you're doing," he mumbles, shaking his head.

I turn away from him and sit back down at the breakfast nook. I nervously sip the champagne. "I'm not doing anything. I'm *hungry*."

He chuckles. "Well then, you will *eat*, my dear, and then we will celebrate." He starts to saunter back my way and I feel my wall going back up. There's another knock at the door. Xavier stops in his tracks again, turning around resentfully, making a low, annoyed sound in the back of his throat. He walks back to the door, opening it bitterly.

He nods at Xavier. "Dahlia, my dear, here you are!" Giorgios strides over to me, handing me the menu. "I recommend the Pasticcio, it's excellent here," he nudges me, winking.

"The Pasticcio? That sounds delicious. I'll take it," I smile.

"Excellent!" Giorgios claps his hands together. "I'll get that started. Anything for you, Mr. Daniels?"

Xavier shakes his head. "No, thank you," he says, as politely as he can.

"Okay, we'll send it up as soon as possible!" Giorgios nods at us both and rushes towards the door.

"Oh, and Giorgios?" I prompt.

"Yes, Dahlia?" he turns, ridiculously attentive.

"I'll be ordering dessert, too," I smirk. I feel Xavier stiffen beside me without even having to look to confirm it.

"Lovely! I'll await your order!" He enthuses.

"Thank you," I smile.

"My pleasure, Mrs. Daniels. *Anything* you need, just ring," he reminds me.

"I will," I smile.

He nods and then lets himself out.

Xavier is suddenly beside me. "Stop playing *games* with me, Violet. I don't *like* it," he growls.

"I'm *not*. *You* said this is our honeymoon. I'm *enjoying* it." I get up, walking past him and uncover the silver lid containing the strawberries. I pluck one out and dip it in the cream provided. Xavier turns and watches me. Lust is coating his eyes and my bravery is dissipating.

"You wouldn't want to eat too much on our honeymoon, dear. It might effect your figure." His eyes rake up my body, greedily.

I fume inwardly, he wants a reaction out of me. "I didn't think it would matter, since I'm already *pregnant*," I spit out, unable to fully contain myself.

Xavier ambles over and stands behind me. My heartbeat picks up again. Adrenaline pumps through me. His hands slide up my arms, causing goosebumps. They land on my shoulders and then go even higher, until his hands are gently grasping my neck. My heart hammers in my chest.

"This *is* going to be an unforgettable evening," he threatens, whispering the words into my ear.

CHAPTER NINETEEN

Monster

"You can't stay in there all night, my love." Xavier croons from the other side of the door.

I don't know if he's a sadist or just plain crazy, but I *know* he's enjoying scaring me a little too much to be *normal*. Who was I kidding? He *wasn't* normal. I'd been hiding in the bathroom for three hours now and I think he was starting to finally lose his patience. I took the longest bath ever in a feeble hope to get away from him. I was already pruny enough, but I used the only idea I had left. I changed into the bikini I had packed.

I open the door slowly. "Can we go for a swim?"

Xavier's eye twitches. "Right *now?* It's three a.m." He's standing dangerously close to my face and I'm anticipating the chance of him, without notice, grabbing me in a not so nice way.

"*So?* The pool is gorgeous. And this is my first and probably *only* time in Greece," I remind him, trying to smile brightly.

He leans on the doorjamb, mulling it over in his head. I know what he's thinking, all of the different possibilities of me trying to escape and all of the scenarios of him stopping it from happening. He becomes distracted from his thought process when his eyes rake over the sight of me in my bikini. His eyes look charged. *Shit.*

"I love that bikini on you," he murmurs. "We could always swim tomorrow?" he suggests.

"Thank you, but I really want to swim right now," I bravely push past him and walk to the balcony that's overlooking the moonlit sea. The rocky cliffs beneath our balcony would definitely not make for a smooth escape, I note. If I look to the left of me, I can see the pool from here. It's lit up, in all its glory, light blue and shimmering.

Xavier comes behind me and wraps his arms around me, gently laying them on top of my shoulders, his hands clasping together over my stomach. I internally curse at myself for flinching when he did that. I am trying my hardest to pull this off. He nestles his chin into the crook of my neck. His lips brush against the tender skin there as he speaks. "Okay, Mrs. Daniels. What my baby *wants*, my baby *gets*." He kisses my neck softly. My skin feels like it's going numb. But to my relief, he releases me. I watch him as he gets his suitcase and starts undressing, in front of me. When he notices me watching him, he smiles smugly. I look away and start puttering around the room, looking anywhere but at him. At last he says, "ready." I look up to spy him in his swim trunks with a towel wrapped lazily around his neck.

Ten minutes later, we're at the pool. The staff didn't even find it strange that we wanted to swim at this hour. Luckily for me, the pool is open twenty-four hours. They're used to tourists swimming at all hours. The pool is vacant, except for a few staff members, who walk around, refilling towels and rolling around dumpsters. I turn to the view of sleeping Santorini and try my best to not lose my breath. It is so gorgeous. The pool is outside, uncovered and in full view of the unspoiled beauty.

"Aren't you going to swim, my love?" Xavier calls from behind me.

I feel like my invisible hackles turn up at the sound of his voice. I turn around. He's already in the pool, his wet hair slicked back. His golden eyes watch me closely. *Is he afraid I'm going to make a move already?* I try not to stare at his perfect Adonis body, glistening in the glow of the moonlight.

"Of course." I walk back and dip my toe in the pool. The water is warm and I'm grateful, because the ocean breeze is crisp and cool. I ease into the water, having no actual desire to swim at the moment. I move towards Xavier in the water, careful to keep just enough distance to avoid any kind of intimacy. "So gorgeous here," I comment, for the sake of making conversation.

"Aren't you going to wet your hair?" Xavier asks, seductively.

I know it isn't a question. He *wants* me to. I must comply with these small, insignificant things to avoid setting him off. This I've learned about him. I duck my whole body into the water, trying as hard as I can not to look alluring. When I resurface, wiping away the water from my eyes, I realize it didn't work.

His eyes glitter darkly. "That's better."

I delicately swallow the lump in my throat. "I'm going to do a few laps," I inform him, before he has his chance to go in for the kill. Before I have the chance to study his expression or hear a word of objection, I break into a swim. I swim back and forth in the pool, doing laps, as Xavier lounges by the steps. I catch glimpses of him sitting there a few times when my head surfaces above the water. He looks as if he's merely waiting for me to tire myself out. *Damn it.* My plan has backfired, yet again. *Where the hell did all the staff go?* I'm running out of time. When I'm out of breath, I come to a stop in the middle of the pool.

Xavier calls to me. "Are you done?"

I look around and spot the hot tub. "I want to get in the hot tub," I call.

Xavier shakes his head in the slightest motion. "Haven't you had *enough* water?"

I pause. "*Please?*"

He sighs and mutters something in Spanish, it doesn't sound pleasant.

I hope I'm not making it worse for me, if this doesn't work out.

Xavier gets out as I make my way to the steps. "I'm going to the bathroom," he announces, turning and glaring at me with a pointed look. "Be right back."

I nod. He wraps a towel around himself and walks away. As soon as he turns the corner, I thrust myself forward to the steps. I emerge from the pool and quickly wrap a towel around myself, water is dripping down my legs and down my back. I run down the concrete stairs that lead towards the outside of the hotel, barefoot. My nerves are as frazzled as my thoughts, as I make my way around the perimeter of the hotel. I had the awful, itchy, unnerving feeling crawling up my neck, that I'm already too late. He's going to get me, I can *feel* it. My hands grip along the white plaster walls as I go, scraping my palms slightly. This hotel is styled like a maze and I feel like the mouse trying to escape. I turn a corner and run smack into a man's body. My heart slams in my chest like brakes in a car, thinking it's Xavier. But to my delight, it's Giorgios.

"Dahlia, are you *alright?* You look like you've seen a ghost. Are you *sick?* Do you need a medic? Where is Mr. Daniels? Why would he leave you out here at this hour of night to fend for *yourself?*" Giorgios pawns over me.

Breathless, I try to communicate effectively. "Giorgios, *listen* to me. Xavier, he isn't my husband, he's holding me against my will. He's going to *kill* me," I pant.

Giorgios' eyes bug out of his head and then I hear the *'click'*.

Dead silence ensues for half a second, before Giorgios lifts his arms slowly and gulps. Xavier is standing behind him, his body hidden in a dark shadow, except for the top of his wet, wavy hair that's barely peeking over Giorgios' head. He must've snuck up behind him, from around the corner. My heart stutters and I start to sweat. Of course he found me.

Xavier moves to stand beside Giorgios, moving the silencer to the side of his head. His eyes are wilder than I've ever seen. "Sorry, baby."

"For wha—"

Before I finish my question, Xavier pulls the trigger. Giorgios' body falls limp and Xavier pushes him off the ledge in one swift motion. I watch Giorgios' body plummet past the cliffs and into the ocean, the way a dying bird falls from the sky.

I don't even realize that I'm screaming until Xavier is back at my side. He grabs me from behind, pulling my body aside, slamming me against the wall. He covers my mouth with his hands. Only, he's holding something white in them now, a cloth? The almost sweet smell permeates into my nose. I register vaguely that it's chloroform. My vision gets fuzzy. "Now if you behave like a *good* girl, no one else will have to die," Xavier admonishes me. I try to fight back, but my body gives way to the chemical.

Xavier isn't just deadly, he's a monster.

CHAPTER TWENTY
Cliff Diving

I wake up with a pounding headache. For one sweet moment, I think I'm back home in my bed. I come to my senses after my eyes squint open and I see that I'm still at the Santorini Princess. I'm still with *him*.

A figure crosses my line of sight, then comes to sit next to me. He sits on the bed where I lie, his back facing me. "I don't like having to kill unnecessary people, Violet," Xavier says quietly. "Now you know the poor decisions you make, can lead to people getting hurt." He turns his head slightly to look at me. His gaze lingers on my body, trailing from my breasts and landing on my ankles. He reaches down and rubs the ankle closest to him. I follow his hand, fear penetrating me like a knife. I'm bound to the bed. "I think you'll stay put better like this," he sighs. He gets up and walks towards the bathroom. "I'm going to take a shower, when I get out we're going to make love," he calls.

I try to get up and bounce back onto the bed. My hands are tied down, too, by cable ties. I scream but the sound is muffled, he's taped my mouth with duct tape.

"Save your energy, darling. You're going to *need* it." Xavier calls from the bathroom.

I buck and thrash my body around wildly on the bed. I'm still wearing my bikini, it won't be much of a challenge for him to take advantage of me. My heart races and the anger builds inside of me, filling me to the brim. Angry, helpless tears form in my eyes. I search the room for something to cut the cable ties with but all that surrounds me is plush pillows and blankets. All too soon Xavier has returned. He ambles over, his wet hair curly and dripping. He's only wearing a white towel wrapped around his waist, it doesn't leave much to the imagination.

"Right where I left you," his eyes twinkle. "Now where were we? Ah, yes." He drops the towel.

Even *I* can't not look at the enormous erection he has on full display. *Sadist*, I think. *Definitely a sadist.*

He climbs on top of me, crawling over me, then he lies next to me. His erection is digging into my hip as he smiles at me, like nothing bad has happened. Like what's happening is perfectly normal. Like he didn't *kill* Giorgios right in front of me. He reaches up to peck me on the lips, peeling back the tape by the corner for access. I *don't* kiss him back. My mind is too busy, reeling with ways to get away. He replaces the tape, smoothing it back over my mouth, which is now burning from the action.

"It would be a waste if we didn't make *full* use of this spectacular bed, don't you think?"

I stare at him. He reaches down and gingerly pulls the tie at one side of my bikini bottoms. I gasp softly, trying to contain the sound. He smiles up at me and watches my face as he reaches over and does the same to the other side. Then he reaches underneath my back and unties the bikini top from behind. "I think it's time to get rid of this silly, little bikini, don't you?" he asks, huskiness filling his voice like the murky green water of a lake. I scrunch my eyes shut as he slides off the bottom and then the top, like they were made of paper. He grips my thighs almost roughly and makes a low grunt noise in the back of his throat. "That's better." My whole body feels hot as Xavier feasts his eyes on my nakedness.

I keep my eyes closed, wishing like Dorothy, I could click together my heels and go back home. But that's impossible, my ankles being bound apart by the cable ties. I feel Xavier climb on top of me. My heart beats fast and loud. He peels back the tape again and kisses my mouth, which I keep taut. When he tries once more, I turn my head away, at least there's *one* thing I can keep from him. He replaces the tape afterward, my lips stinging even more from the friction. My lack of enthusiasm doesn't deter him though. He kisses me hungrily down my jaw line and neck. Then he gropes my breasts in his hands, teasing each one slowly with his tongue. He takes his time lavishing each one before grazing his fingers down my stomach and in between my legs. I try to clench myself together, but my legs are impossibly spread, it does no good. He rubs me slowly, over and over until my traitorous body responds. I feel the wetness between my legs and hate myself for it.

"Stop trying to fight your attraction for me, Violet." Xavier murmurs. Suddenly his mouth is on my stomach, he licks his way down and I know where he's heading. "Let me just have a small taste," he whispers. His mouth meets with the most sensitive part of in between my legs and I buck upward. I mentally curse myself. *Lie still and it'll be over sooner*, I think. He's enjoying this too much. But he just leans back momentarily, chuckles and returns to his work. He licks over and over, relentlessly, until I fall apart. I try to stifle the moans that escape, but it's harder than I thought. The tingling sensation runs from my waist to my toes, causing goosebumps all over my body. I felt so guilty, being pleasured by someone that I'm purely terrified of. But Xavier had the upper hand, he knew my body and my weak points. He knew how to please me expertly. I had the feeling he knew how to please *all* women expertly. "See that wasn't so bad, was it?" I felt him crawl on top of me and thought about trying my best to fight him off. *What if that just got him off more though and he was rougher with me?* I didn't want him to *hurt* me. Fear abruptly spiked back in my heart. *What if he kills me after this?* I thought, suddenly. After seeing what he did today, I didn't have a doubt in my mind that he was capable of it. My eyes shot open just in time to see him settle himself in between my legs. "So you want to *watch* now?" he teased. "*Watch,*" he challenged. He slowly pushed his large length inside of me, filling me. I closed my eyes again. But blinked them back open in shock when I felt an immediate difference. He wasn't wearing a condom. Now, I had one more thing to worry about. Unless he did decide to kill me after all, then I supposed it wouldn't matter.

A few hours later, I wake to find myself alone in the bed. I'm still naked, but my body is covered by a blanket now. My body is sticky and sore from Xavier's earlier assaults on it. *Where was Xavier?* Then I get my answer. I can hear Xavier speaking with what sounds like authorities outside of the door.

"*We'd like to speak with your wife also when she's available.*" I hear them say.

"Of course," Xavier replies. "She's in the shower right now though," he adds.

I think about screaming, but knowing I probably wouldn't be loud enough and remembering Xavier's warning. *"The poor decisions you make, can lead to more people getting hurt."* His words ring in my

Kathey Gray

ears. So I decide to change tack. I look around the room again, this time finding something I can only describe as a God-send. Xavier, in his rush to get the door, left behind something very important on the bedside table. A knife. I stretch my right hand towards it, the plastic cuts into my wrist painfully. I cringe but push my arm harder. My nails graze the handle and it wobbles, almost falling off the table. I start and then listen to the voices outside of the door again. I can still hear Xavier's low baritone from behind it. I try again, more carefully this time. I put my finger underneath the handle, careful not to topple it this time. Then I put another finger and then another until the whole handle rests in my palm. I cautiously turn it the other way in my hand, so that the blade is pointed downward. I slide it slowly in between my wrist and the cable tie, then I twist it around so that the jagged end is pressed up against the hard plastic. I use my fingers to move the knife up and down, sawing away at the plastic. Luckily, the knife is deadly sharp and it doesn't take much to loosen it. I press it hard against the plastic and hear the pop. After that, it's easy to slice off the rest. I rip the tape off of my mouth and grab my bikini off of the floor. I slip it on, opting to keep the knife. I tuck it in the back of my swimsuit top and search for the easiest and fastest way out. *The balcony*. I run over to it and climb over the edge carefully, my feet meeting with the jagged cliff rocks. They dig into the soft pads of my feet. I crouch down and climb until I find one that has a clear landing spot. I stand, preparing to dive. Just then, the image of Giorgios' body flashes through my mind and I

152

shudder. He's probably down there somewhere on the bottom of the ocean.

"*Violet?*" I hear Xavier calling for me.

I turn to see him watching me from inside of the balcony. "Don't jump, Violet. There are sharp rocks down there and you *will* be badly hurt," he steps forward, holding up his hands.

Better than being with you, I think.

I turn back around, staring down at the sharp rocks jutting out of the water. The angry waves crash against them, violently. The water looks freezing. *Would I* get hurt? What if I *die* because of this stunt? But what if I die at the hand of Xavier because I *didn't* jump?

"Violet, sweetheart..." Xavier croons, slowly taking another step. "Don't jump."

I took a deep breath, gathering courage. There was no more time to hesitate, he was coming closer. Suddenly, I heard my mom's voice come into my head. When I was little and I was learning to swim, I was scared to jump into the pool. She waded in the water below me, smiling reassuringly. "*Just close your eyes and jump, honey*," she beckoned me. But that was just a memory, this was *now*. I was hearing her voice *now*, telling me the same thing. "*Just close your eyes and jump, Violet*," she urged.

So I did.

CHAPTER TWENTY-ONE

SOS

"*Violet!!!*" Xavier screamed angrily as my body sailed through the air.

I felt liberated, like a bird soaring, for just a moment. The moment ended quickly as my body lunged downward at a frightening speed. I had done well to avoid landing in the path of the jagged black rocks, but I was still scared to death of the impact. My body sliced into the water before I had time for any more thoughts. The water was as cold as ice. I plunged into the deep, dark ocean for longer than I thought. I went deeper than I thought I would, too. When I finally stopped sinking, I immediately flailed my arms and legs around, fighting to force my body into a lying position rather than face down. I tried to remain calm as I held my breath. I floated upwards and began to swim to the surface. I had no idea where I would come up, but I hoped I had swam further than I thought. I also hoped Xavier wouldn't be waiting for me when I came up. With a smile, or a gun, or both. My lungs felt like they were going to explode as I reached my arms up further and further, grasping for the water's break. Panic began to rattle my brain. *Just how deep had I dove? Surely the surface was near?* I fought, kicking and pushing upward until my hand finally met a breeze. I stuck both hands out of the water then, followed quickly after by my arms and head. I gasped for air, swallowing a huge gulp of it. My arms splashed around noisily and I looked around to check for Xavier's presence. I had somehow ended up on the left side of the hotel, now I was behind another hotel altogether. The Santorini Princess was in view, but my balcony was not. Relieved I quickly began swimming towards the shore, which I had found to be much more rocky for my liking. I hadn't calculated the escape thoroughly enough though and was met with a giant wave that went crashing on top of my head. I got thrown back under, accidentally swallowing a mouthful of saltwater. I swam upwards only to get hit by another wave. My body thrusted back downward yet again, surrounded by bubbles and white foam. The bubbles tickled my skin like a thousand tiny feathers. I pushed my arms upward with great strength and broke through the surface again. I was becoming exhausted and desperate. I could see the shore again, even though the waves had knocked me further than I was before. I began swimming purposely towards it, until I spotted Xavier's figure. My heart halted at the sight of him, waiting for me on the shore. His expression was dark, I could tell all the way from here. The way the sun hit the angles of his cheek bones, I could tell his eyes were narrowed. I immediately turned and started swimming away from his direction, towards the middle of the ocean. I knew I was risking drowning by doing so, but I didn't have a choice. I swam in long strides until I could barely make out his figure. I had swam far away from the crashing waves, this part of the ocean although deeper, was calmer. A small speed boat began to approach and I almost lost it, thinking Xavier had somehow caught up to me already. Until it neared and I spotted a small, balding man. I feared he didn't see me and would hit me at first, until he slowed and turned off the boat's engine.

"Ma'am, are you alright?" he asked in a southern accent.

I knew he must've thought I looked strange all the way out there, in boating territory. Even the surfers didn't stray this far and I didn't even have a board. I stared at the man, measuring his danger level. His accent was clearly American, that was already a good sign. He was wearing a Hawaiian shirt and khaki shorts. He didn't wear glasses or have a creepy mustache, so pedophile was out of the question. Nothing about this man screamed intimidating. I decided to trust him, if only momentarily.

I shivered. "I could use a little help."

"*Sure!* Sure, yes, *by all means.* You looked like you were in trouble out here all by yourself." He beckoned me closer with a wave of his hand. "Do you need me to call the police or something?" he asked quickly, shooting glances left and right.

By then he had extended his hand to me and helped to pull me out of the water and into the boat. He handed me a towel, which I gratefully wrapped around my body. He gazed at me with concerned eyes. White bushy brows furrowed at me.

"Yes, yes I do." I admitted. *Was it finally over? Was someone finally going to save me? Could I finally go home now?*

At my admission, the little man scurried over to his boat radio. "This is Speedy 919. I have a girl here who's in trouble. I need the police at the North dock of the island."

Twenty minutes later I was waiting with 'John' the retired car salesman, at the North dock of the island. He had a wife waiting for him in the hotel next door to ours, and two daughters in college back in Maryland.

"The police will be here shortly," he reassured me.

I nodded. "Thank you, so much, for everything." I hugged the towel around me. I stared at his small boat, now tied up at the dock. The sun was still shining bright, it was barely past noon. Xavier must be close by, I shuddered involuntarily. *The police are coming, the police are coming.* I reminded myself. I was grateful that John didn't want to ask any questions about just what exactly had happened to me, and why I needed help from the police. I figured he was aware of how delicate the situation was, and that it wasn't really his business anyway. It made me feel better that he didn't know, it was safer for *him* if he didn't. The last thing I wanted, was for *more* people to get hurt on my account. Especially not this sweet old man, who rescued me, a perfect stranger, not knowing just how much danger he was putting himself in.

"No problem. There was no way I was going to leave you *out* there, I have two daughters, you know?" he chuckled.

I nodded. Suddenly, it made me remember. "John, can I use your cell phone real quick?"

He fished it out of his pocket. "Of course." He handed it to me and I thanked him, then I quickly typed in my dad's number. As it rang, my nerves felt on edge. *What if he wasn't home?* On the third ring, he finally picked up.

"*Hello?*" His familiar voice filled my heart with warmth.

"Dad!" I choked.

"*Violet?* Violet, where have you been? Are you *alright?* Everyone has been trying to get a *hold of you!* What's *happened?* What's *going on?*" My dad flooded me with questions, his voice a peculiar mix of relief and castigation. I held up a finger at John, who nodded understandably and I walked a few feet away, out of his earshot.

"Dad, I'm *okay*...it's a *long* story. I don't have my phone. The important part is, I'm *coming home*. Xavier...he isn't who I thought he was..." I stopped dead in my tracks, my back going ramrod straight. Something cold and hard was pressed into the middle of my back. I knew what it was immediately and I knew just who it belonged to. "I....love you dad..." I added breathlessly, before the phone slid silently from my palm. It dropped to the sand with a muted thump. Tears welled in my eyes. I should've known it wouldn't be that easy. I slowly lifted my head, dreading what I would find. If I found John dead, my heart wouldn't be able to take it. He was lying in the sand, where I had just seen him standing only moments ago. A strangled sob escaped. I realized that the only weapon I'd thought to bring, the knife from the hotel, was somewhere on the bottom of the ocean now.

"*Shh, shh, calm down*," Xavier soothed, whispering into my ear and smoothing my hair. "He's *alive*, I left him alive for you," he reassured me. "I think it's time for us to move on from Greece though, don't you? Forgive me my love, but we need to move quickly." He lifted the gun from my back and struck it to the side of my temple.

He Loves Me...

CHAPTER TWENTY-TWO

Paris

I wake up with the familiar pounding that I've grown accustomed to, but this time it's accompanied with bruises. I wince as I reach up and brush the tender, swollen skin at my temple. He *pistol whipped me?* I'm lying on a bed somewhere new. I'm not at the Santorini Princess anymore, of that I'm sure. The bed I'm lying in is adorned in rich burgundy and cream hues. My eyes scan the room looking for clues. The decor is romantic, with paintings on the walls and warm lighting. Xavier's sitting at a small iron table, on the balcony outside, the sunset turning his dark figure into a silhouette. He's sipping on a cappuccino, looking completely careless and at ease. Upon my attention, his eyes meet with mine. Something dark glints in them and fear spreads through me all over again. Although I know just how angry he is with me, he attempts to play it off.

"My love, you're awake. Come have a cappuccino with me. The sunsets in France are breathtaking," he urges, in a friendly voice.

The shock that hits me is enough to knock me over. He somehow got my unconscious body all the way to *France?* Maybe this man *is* capable of anything.

I rise stiffly, more compelled to obey him this time than *ever*. I realize I'm wrapped in a plush robe. It falls open, displaying the baby pink satin slip that I don't remember putting on. Of course not, because *he* put it on me. I close the robe back, self consciously, then sit across from him at the table. The breeze is warmer here, but in a pleasant way. He pushes the matching teacup at me, smiling. I lift my shaking hand and carefully take a sip, trying to avoid eye contact. The cappuccino is rich and satisfying, it slowly fills my body with warmth. "T-thank you," I mutter, my nerves causing my voice to tremble.

Xavier's responding grin is unsettling. I turn my attention to the people milling about in the village below. Across the street is a small café and a set of apartments. I can see people sitting at the tables of the café, sipping on cappuccinos much like mine and enjoying French dishes. The street below is just as entertaining to watch. It's filled with small cars, people on mopeds and people riding by with bikes that have baskets, containing fresh bread or paper bags carrying fruits and vegetables. The cozy little scene below me almost makes me forget who I'm with.

"It's lovely here isn't it? I knew you wanted to come back..." he muses. "How's your cappuccino?"

I'm pulled from the peaceful illusion at that question. I stare into the cup, nothing seems amiss. But as I look at him, my vision spins and blurs. My jaw drops slightly. "You...you..." *Poison? Is it poison?* Is he finally *done* with me? If it's poison at least I'll die quickly and without an immense amount of pain. At least I got to tell my dad I loved him. France is a beautiful place to die, I guess.

"Roofied you? Sorry about that. I know I told you I'd never do that." He shakes his head slightly, chuckling. "But you.... you've been a *very* bad girl. You've given me no choice..." he explains. I'm barely listening as his words draw out and echo in my brain. I start to fall to one side but catch myself. Xavier steadies me. "Let's get you back to bed, my love," he smiles. He moves over to me and scoops me into his arms. He carries me back to the bed, pressing his lips against mine. I have the awful feeling that he isn't just going to lie me down.

I wake much later, by the looks of the darkness surrounding me. I'm relieved that I'm not tied up or bound this time. I reach between my legs because I *have* to know. My panties are missing and my hand meets with wetness. I can't *believe* he really did. I don't know why his actions keep surprising me, maybe because I thought he was such a good guy when I first met him. Or maybe he was never a good guy and I failed to see the warning signs. Maybe he preyed upon women like me, innocent, vulnerable women. *Stupid* women. I had stupidly ran right into his arms, all because of his good lucks and shining exterior. Who *wouldn't* though? Probably Ava. She was much smarter than me. Definitely not Fiona...she'd probably be loving every minute of this insane debauchery. But no, Ava, she knew there was something wrong. She'd sensed it and tried to warn me. Now, here I was, on the run with an ex-drug cartel operator, killer, dangerous criminal, rapist, sadist, abuser and oh yeah, he's my fiancé. I was running out of ideas and time probably. Is *this* what happened to Trinity? Did he treat *her* like this? Is she even *alive?* If so, she's probably hiding out for the rest of her life from Xavier. I slowly moved my limbs, being absolutely dumbfounded that he'd left me unrestrained and unsupervised. Maybe he underestimated the potency of the drug? I sat up and my head swam, I held it in my hands to steady the swirling of the room. I slid my legs slowly off the edge of the bed and stood carefully. I looked around once more, not finding Xavier anywhere. I walked slowly to the still opened balcony and peered out. The street was still crawling with people, mostly the late night clubbers and prostitutes, not the most savory of characters. The night crowd was much different than the day time crowd. But the Eiffel Tower was visible and breathtaking lit up in all its dazzling delight. I couldn't let its beauty deter me for long though. I had to get back to the matter at hand. *Escaping.* I tip toed back into the room and quietly surveyed every corner and even the bathroom. Xavier was *gone.* My heart started pounding quickly in my chest as I ran to my suitcase to get actual clothes. I don't how wearing underwear felt like a luxury, but it did. While I was sifting though the clothes, something fell from one of my high heels. It was the ones Fiona had let me borrow that night I went to Xavier's party to tell him "goodbye". I recognized it immediately, it was the card that detective had given me on the first occasion I was "fleeing" from Xavier. *Soloman Jacobs*...I could only take it as a another sign from the heavens. I held the card tight in my palm and ran to the phone beside the bed. I dialed the operator before punching in Soloman's number.

It rang and rang and rang and then..

"Detective Soloman Jacobs, here" His voice sounded far away, seeing how I *was* calling from a very long distance away.

"Solomon! I- I don't know if you remember me...you gave me this card and told me to call you if I ever needed help and...well, I need help. My name is—"

"Violet Crenshaw," he said with familiarity.

"Well...yes..." *How did the hell did he know it was me? "How did you?"*

"I'm a detective, remember?"

"Oh, well that makes sense. I'm sort of in a bind and I'd really like your help. Please."

"Where are you? And what sort of 'bind' exactly?"

I grabbed a menu off of the bedside table and read off the address. "31 Avenue George V, Paris, France. At the Four Seasons Hotel George V."

"Wait— you're in Paris? Why the hell didn't you say so sooner? I don't know if I'll be able to help you...I'm sorry. I can contact my connections in France and see what they can do—"

"Please, it *has* to be you," I interrupted, adamant. I was too afraid to let my *one* connection to the U.S. that could actually *help* me, slip through my fingers. "You're my *only* chance..." I pleaded with him.

"It's him again, isn't it? The man you were running from the first time? You're with him?"

"Yes and he's *very dangerous*. He may *kill me* and *soon*. He killed..." I sobbed, unable to say Giorgios' name. I was unable to even speak.

"Give me a name. What's his name?" Solomon demanded, his voice threatening and serious. I knew

what he meant, he wanted Xavier's name, not the men he killed...at least not yet.

"Xavier Daniels," I whispered.

"*I'm coming,*" is all Soloman had to say.

But I wasn't alone anymore. I *felt* his presence before I actually *saw* him standing there. He had a murderous expression on his face.

"*Who* are you talking to?" he yelled, causing me to flinch.

I slammed the phone back down on the receiver, effectively hanging up on Soloman.

Xavier stepped closer, pointing at me, accusatory. "You were *talking* to the police, *weren't you?*"

I looked down, avoiding the scary glow in his eyes that had nothing to do with love and more to do with excitement in the pain he was undoubtedly going to inflict upon me as soon as I muttered the wrong answer. The trick is, there was no "right" one.

"I— I was just talking to Ava...she can't *believe* I'm in *France*.." I laughed once and attempted to force my frown upward into a small, curved smile.

"*Liar*..." Xavier stepped closer. He looked down at me, towering over me. Sweat was beginning to bead underneath his golden curls on his forehead. His eyes were so scary, the pupils appeared to be enlarged. Something shifted then, inside of me. I was tired of him cornering me like a puppy who disobeyed his master. *I wasn't his fucking puppy.* We'd already played this game before, and from what I gathered, I was about to lose. I was *tired* of losing.

He suddenly crouched down and grabbed me by the back of my head, holding my hair tight. He stared me in the eyes. "*Tell me* who you were talking to, you *lying bitch!*" he spit, each word dripping with acid.

This time I didn't flinch. I barely blinked. I looked him dead in the eye, ignoring his question. "Who's *Trinity?*"

Xavier looked like he'd seen a ghost. Perhaps he had. His pupils shrank and he let go of my hair and pulled away.

I took advantage of his moment of weakness. "You talk about her in your sleep, you know. She must've been someone very special to you..."

Xavier's eyes were grave but at least he didn't look as angry. His jaw set and strained. Just then the phone rang. The shrill, eerie sound filled the room that was already so weighted with darkness. Our eyes met, before we both reached for it at the same time. But Xavier pushed me away easily with one hand and held me against the wall by my neck.

"Hello?"

There was a pause.

"I said *hello?*" He waited.

"Who the *fuck* is this?" He spat. Then he slammed down the receiver. *But who had called? Was it Soloman?*

Xavier was visibly shaken by the call, or maybe it was me bringing up Trinity's name. He released me and wiped the sweat off of his forehead with the back of his hand, then turned to glare at me. He was getting sick of me, I could tell. My time was almost up. I shuddered as I recalled how easily he had disposed of Giorgios, without a second thought.

"Get up," he urged, grabbing me roughly by the arm.

He pulled me off of the wall easily and I stumbled along, scared once more. *What did he mean to do with me? Was it already over?* An awful helpless feeling overtook my body and I stumbled even slower, my legs feeling like they were suddenly knee deep in sand. No, *No!* I couldn't let the fear paralyze me! I had to act, I had to defend myself! My eyes started scanning the room for weapons. But Xavier only opened the bathroom door, threw me in, and slammed it shut again, locking it. Maybe he just couldn't stand to look at me right now? I waited though, with bated breaths for a few moments just to be sure. When he didn't return after that, and I heard the TV click on, I knew I was safe for the evening. At least I hoped. But here I was again, the puppy put away for misbehaving. I sighed and reached to gather the hotel room towels, making myself a makeshift cot on the floor.

I woke to the sound of the bathroom door opening and I sat up alarmed. Xavier walked in, looking much more composed. I shriveled into the corner and watched as he set down a tray next to me, filled with food. I glanced at the tray and then him again, suspicious.

"Don't worry, I didn't roofie it this time. I thought you should have something to eat. We'll be leaving France in the morning and you'll need to be well fed for the long journey," he explained.

I stared down at the tray again. The food was mouthwatering. It was some sort of chicken dish with vegetables. There was a side of fresh baked bread and a bottle of wine, uncorked, a wine glass turned upside down beside it. I wasn't sure I *could* avoid eating it, even if it *was* poisoned or drugged.

"Enjoy," Xavier smiled, then turned and walked back out, locking the door once more.

As I scarfed down the food, I couldn't help but think of his words. "We're leaving France..." and "long journey". I hoped that didn't mean anything much worse for me. But wait, I *couldn't* leave France. Soloman was coming for me and he was my last hope! I'd have to divert him somehow...or get away. But my body trembled as I recalled the *last* time I got away. Xavier made sure I payed for it. The next time, I figured, would be much worse. No, I couldn't leave France, there was no way.

CHAPTER TWENTY-THREE
Room Service

"Time to go." A deep voice ordered.

I startled awake to find Xavier staring down at me, somberly. I stared at his fuzzy figure in the bathroom doorway with confusion. It was *morning* already? *But I had accidentally fallen asleep when I was supposed to be making a plan!* That food tired me out and satisfied me too much. *I was out of time!* I rose stiffly to my feet, apprehension clear in my posture. Xavier stuck his arm through mine, crooking us together.

"Where's my stuff?" I asked, looking into the room at the made up bed. I noticed that it was still dark outside, with not even a hint of blue to indicate the morning sun was on its way. It must've been two or three in the morning. I was right to assume that I hadn't slept much. The last few days had been such a whirlwind and not in the way I'd *ever* imagine my "honeymoon" going. Not that I *had* ever imagined it.

173

"I already have it in the car," he said shortly. "Put your shoes on," he ordered in a low voice.

His manner had changed from frustrated to deadly in a matter of hours. He shoved me in the direction of my sandals and I felt his tense muscles. I sat on the bed and strapped them on. I was moving deliberately slow though, still trying to come up with a plan. "Hurry up," he said in a deadly quiet voice.

When I finished, he grabbed my arm hard, bruising the soft skin with his steel grip. He led me out of the door, shutting it quickly. Then he crooked our arms together again, in a more amiable pose, the way that lovers do. He hurried me along down the vast hallway with rich carpeted floors. I scanned the halls for something, anything, that might be my answer out of this. But no one was around. Everyone was asleep in their rooms by now. Surely that was why he picked this time. We began to approach a small cart holding silver lidded dishes. The dishes were dirty and had been placed in the hallway outside of the occupant's door on purpose, for the hotel staff to come pick up. Down the hall, there was an elevator. But we were about to turn into another hall, probably leading to another elevator, one closer to where Xavier had a car waiting. A car waiting to take me from France to God knows where. I saw the light above the elevator indicate that it was about to open..someone was about to exit. A plan formed quickly in my mind. If the timing would work just right, this was my chance. I slowed my pace and Xavier's hand tugged on mine.

"What are you doing?" Xavier muttered, irritated, barely containing his ever growing hostility towards me.

"There's something stuck in my shoe," I pretended to limp. He stopped, reluctantly, pausing to allow me to inspect it. Pausing right next to those silver lidded dishes, he loosened his grip on my arm. He held only my wrist now, in his vice-like grip. I crouched down and fiddled with the inside of the sole under my foot, digging for the invisible invader. The elevator dinged. My free hand shot out, grabbing one of the heavy silver lids. I stood and swiftly jabbed it upward at Xavier's face. He abruptly let go of my hand, crying out in pain. I didn't pause to look this time. I broke into a full sprint for the elevator doors. I could feel Xavier following behind me, I could hear his footfalls quietly thudding on the luxurious carpeting. But I couldn't afford a glance back. The elevator doors opened, revealing the sole occupant. A young hipster with a mop of dark, curly hair and earbuds in. He nodded his head along to the music, never lifting his eyes from his IPhone. I ran into the elevator, pushing him aside. Xavier was hot on my tail, two steps away. The boy looked at me, awakened from his technology stupor.

"*Sorry,*" I mouthed at him, then pushed him hard out of the elevator and onto Xavier.

I pressed close on the door and watched as Xavier began to scramble back to his feet. The elevator doors closed and my brief fit of adrenaline was replaced with pure terror. Liquid, gold, pure terror. *What have I done? He's going to kill me! What am I going to do now?* I suddenly felt the weight of being completely alone and the anxiety it held. He's not going to hurt that boy now, *is he?* Surely he won't have time, because he'll be chasing *me.* The elevator suddenly lit up on the second floor, indicating it was going to stop there, on its way to the lobby. I felt the fear choking me. What if it's Xavier....? *Had he caught up to me already?* I couldn't even breathe correctly, *how* could I attempt to *fight* him off? The fear was almost paralyzing as I waited for those doors to open. But when they did there was only a portly French maid.

She smiled at me with warmth and small, pleasant brown eyes. She was the opposite of intimidating in a pale, yellow dress with a frilly white apron. "*Bonjour!*" she said warmly.

"Bonjour," I repeated, a little breathless. She smiled as she squeezed her cart in beside me. But Xavier suddenly emerged on the opposite end of the hallway, from the stairwell, no doubt. I knew if he got into the elevator with us, it'd be too easy for him to trap me once more. I pushed my way out of the elevator.

"Excuse me," I said politely, in English instead of French.

But the maid nodded anyway. Xavier was running towards me as soon as the doors closed. I darted off down another hallway, one in a darker wing of the hotel. I clung to the shadows that hung on the walls and slipped inside a door that was already ajar. I pulled it to, but not quite shut, unsure of what kind of room it was and if there were occupants. I hid behind the door, waiting. I heard quiet footsteps approach and I held my breath as the door I was hiding behind, opened slowly, pinning me further against the back of the wall. My heart was racing dangerously fast and I felt lightheaded enough to pass out. I fought to hold on to control. The light in the room suddenly flicked on, casting light upon all of the shadows, except me. I was still safely obscured in the shadow behind the door. I suppressed a gasp, as I saw the large feet from underneath the door. The silence was maddening. I heard a strange scrape suddenly, against the door. The sound was unnerving and eerie all at once. My heart leaped into my throat. The scraping started low at the bottom of the door, scraping its way up, stopping next to my face. Then it stopped completely. I felt like I could hear my breath, it was so heavy and panic filled. Surely he could hear my heartbeat drumming loudly and hotly in my ears. Without warning, a ten inch machete sunk into the wooden door, two inches from my face. The wood splintered around it. I couldn't help the blood curdling scream that ensued.

CHAPTER TWENTY-FOUR

Free

The knife was yanked back out of the door, leaving a huge slice through it. Xavier swung open the door, looking much more calm than I was comfortable with, for someone with blood running down his nose and onto his shirt. It was a deadly calm. "You ever play that game seven minutes in heaven, baby?"

I stared back at him, frightened and confused.

"Because we're about to play it."

He grabbed me by the back of my neck and drug me out from behind the door. I was about to scream, I took a deep breath and filled my lungs with air. But I held the breath I took, when Xavier pressed the blade of the knife against my throat.

"That's *right*, you keep quiet now," he murmured with pleasure.

He walked behind me, urging me along. "Now, I thought after all we've been through, that you'd remember the little *talk* we had about your behavior," he scolded. I took slow, careful steps, scanning the room around me. Turns out, it was a larger, unoccupied suite. It must've been reserved for the wealthiest of guests, by the looks of it. There were actually two connected rooms, one was still dark inside, though the door was open. Xavier started pushing me towards it. I couldn't help but whimper a little, I didn't want to die in that room, or a closet. My eyes frantically searched for something that might help me, but Xavier covered my eyes with his other hand.

"*Nu-uh*, no peeking."

He guided me through the dark, steering me, until we reached the closet. I knew we were in it because the sound of silence somehow muted even more. There was no air supply in this closet. Silent tears streamed down my face. Xavier lifted his hands from my eyes. We were standing in a small closet full of folded linens. The light was on, but it didn't provide much comfort, only clues. Xavier turned to face me, pressing me against the wall of the closet. Hangers tangled in my hair. He slid the knife in his back pocket, but not before I could see the smear of blood on the edge of the blade. He *had* cut me, enough to draw blood. I was relieved when he put it away, even if it was only temporarily.

"You know the rules," his eyes glittered. "I can do *whatever* I want to you for seven minutes," he taunted.

His hands lowered to his belt, which he unbuckled and slid off. I gulped involuntarily and he smiled. Then he lifted the belt, wrapped it around my neck and tightened it, like a noose. I gasped louder then. He reached slowly between my legs, slipping off my panties. Then he quickly unzipped his own pants, all the while keeping a hand on the strap of the belt, making sure I wasn't going anywhere. I felt him against me, hard as steel. My eyes were searching again, but then I remembered, his knife in his back pocket. Surely he'll be too occupied to protect it properly.

"Now, I'm going to fuck you, however I want and if you resist," he pulled against the strap hard to prove a point. I choked for air as the thick leather crushed my throat, blocking all air from traveling through. Then he released me and I gulped for air, leaning over a little. He pushed me back, uncaring. He lifted my leg, wrapping it around his waist. He positioned himself at my entrance and plunged into me with a sharp thrust that made me cry out in pain. I had to focus though, I had to let him get close enough to the edge for my opportunity. He thrusted into me roughly again and again, I cried out every time. And every time, he tightened the strap around my neck a little more. I was barely able to strain for air when I could tell his finish was near. He loosened the belt strap the tiniest bit, too lost in the feelings, and I leaned forward, sliding the knife from his back pocket swiftly. I didn't hesitate, I drove the knife straight through his back. Xavier's eyes went wide and he dropped the strap.

"Mi amor, *what* have you *done?*" He stumbled back a few steps, staggering.

I kicked him hard in the stomach and he fell over, groaning in pain. I hastily opened the door and ran through the dark room and into the room that was lit up. I was halfway through, when Xavier gripped my ankle causing me to fall. I landed on my hands and knees, as he tried to drag me back. "I haven't got my full seven minutes," he spat, threatening me.

I turned to look at him, he was weak and bleeding a lot now. "And you're not *going* to!" I kicked him square in the nose again. He released my ankle, screaming, and I ran like hell. I ran down hallway after hallway, until I found an elevator. I punched the elevator door button repeatedly, checking behind me between every push. Prints of blood dotted the buttons. The elevator door opened and I ran in. The doors closed excruciatingly slow and I watched as the button lights, decreased in number, until finally at the lobby level.

The doors opened and I ran out, running straight into a man dressed in burgundy. He groped my arms, sturdily. A glass-shattering scream escaped me. "Miss? Tout va bien? Avez-vous besoin d'aide?" He asked in French. It was one of the concierge's. He was a thin, young man with dark curly hair, kind brown eyes and thick eyebrows. When I wobbled to the side and fell into the man's arms, he called to the other employees of the hotel. "Aidez-moi!! Nous avons besoin d'aide!!!"

Everyone was a flutter in the lobby suddenly. Making phone calls and rushing to help me. Arriving and departing guests were told to stay where they were. My eyes could barely focus. "Police, I need the police," I finally muttered.

The man looked down at me. "Oui, nous sommes obetinar la police, madam," he nodded reassuringly, lips tight. I must've looked alarming to him. I was still wearing my robe and satin pink gown, now covered in blood, with Xavier's belt still wrapped around my neck.

"He's still up there you know, on the second floor," I offered, weakly. Tears were pouring down my face now. Exhaustion and relief taking control of my emotions.

The man nodded and yelled to the others. The men in red ran to the elevators and some took the stairs. I closed my eyes, it was *over*. It was *finally* over.

CHAPTER TWENTY-FIVE
Pittsburgh

I don't remember falling asleep, but I awoke in the hospital. I felt a firm grip on my shoulder and gasped, a deep ragged breath.

"*Violet*, Violet— you're okay. It's *okay* now," a rich voice soothed. The blur of tears in my eyes cleared enough for me to see the face of Detective Soloman Jacobs staring at me.

"You *came*," I choked out.

"Of course I came," he seemed offended. "I told you I would."

"Did they find him?" I gulped, my throat ached from the action. It felt like it was bruised. My hand twitched, wanting to reach up and touch it, but I managed to keep it down in front of the detective. "Did they find Xavier?"

The detective strolled around my bed and took a seat, sighing. "They're out there looking for him now."

My heart halted for what seemed like long enough to kill me. "You mean...you mean...they *didn't*..." I felt my chest constrict and I began to hyperventilate. He's out there, *loose*. They didn't *catch* him. He could be *anywhere*. He could be *here*. *What if he was coming for me?* I thought about the knife I left in his back. How is he even *alive?* Is his breed of dangerous just *un-killable?*

"Violet..." Detective Jacobs reached out and gently laid his hand atop mine. His eyes were warm and soothing. "You're *safe*. Don't worry— this will all be over in no time," he reassured me. But I didn't *feel* reassured.

"Do you think you're well enough to answer some questions?"

I nodded. He nodded too and let go of my hand.

Anything I could do to speed this process along, I thought. I answered all of his questions.

I found out that Xavier had somehow flown my unconscious body from Greece to France on a private, stolen plane, and had somehow gotten me into the hotel undetected. His real name was Diego Maldanado and was on several most wanted lists.

Including the U.S. and Mexico. He was the number one suspect in the murder of his ex-fiancée, Trinity Fields, who'd been dead for two years. She had been strangled to death. The mute thud of my heart was accompanied with realization at those words. He was the head of a major drug cartel in Mexico for eight years and was wanted for several crimes there, including murder. I felt numb as I listened on, realizing I'd been in danger all along. I had no idea how much at the time. I was too blinded by Xavier's persuasive charm and devilishly good looks. What kind of luck did I have, that *this* was my first relationship? I swore off dating right then and there. I'd rather be alone.

"Now, that you're awake and you're okay, the medical examiners will need to come... gather their data," Soloman said lowly, in a meditative voice.

I felt my body tense up and it must've shown on my face, too.

"They have to do a thorough investigation of all the evidence," he explained, putting a hand behind his neck. "You want him behind bars, don't you?"

I nodded, slowly, fighting back tears. I was so embarrassed, so ashamed that he had done this to me. That I'd *let* him do this to me.

"Violet," Soloman called. I looked up. "This isn't your fault, you *know* that right? Diego's a bad man and bad men don't belong on the streets. Let's put him away, *okay?*"

"Okay," I agreed.

I was released from the hospital the next day. I couldn't believe how *relieved* I was to leave France. Such a romantic, enchanting place, had been forever tainted to me now. The flight back was strange, I still wasn't used to my freedom. I was allowed to go by myself to the bathroom, and wander around the airport shops. I fought the urge to flinch every time Soloman raised his hand to reach for something or simply scratch his neck. I was skittish and on edge still. They still hadn't found Diego, after searching the whole hotel. All they had found was a trail of blood leading from the hotel room to the stairwell. After that it had disappeared. Police had scoured the streets with little progress. The only lead they had was an old woman who had been walking her dog on the street. She claimed she had seen a man that looked like Diego at the dock renting a boat. Only, his hair had been shorter and darker. Police suspected he had somehow found a quick way to change his identity. I felt worried that he may meet another woman on his way, and become a new person to her. That he would lure her, as he had me. But I hoped that he'd be too busy running from the police to bother with any new conquests. I did feel safe though, traveling alongside with Soloman. He had let me use his phone to call my dad. Turns out he and Ava had been searching for me since my first call to her from the airport. I felt bad that he was crying, but better when I knew it was with relief. I apologized to him over and over again, telling him how much I loved him. He kept telling me how happy he was, how proud he was of me and that he would be waiting for me at the airport. The next call was harder. After Ava yelled at me for what seemed like forever, she finally broke down and cried too. I had to apologize all over again. It all felt like a dream, because surely I couldn't make it out of there *alive*. Surely I couldn't get *away* from him. But here I was, alive and finally on my way back home. Tears slid down my cheeks silently, as I slid off Xavier's engagement ring and put it in my pocket. I'd be pawning it as soon as I got back home. Soloman politely ignored my quiet sobs of relief and gratitude.

When we finally touched down in Pittsburgh, it felt like the veil lifted over my eyes. I was doing all I could to not push everyone out of the way. When I finally broke through the crowd, my dad and Ava were there. I ran to them, forgetting all about Soloman briefly. I hugged my dad hard, crying onto his shoulder. He patted me on the back and sniffed too, endearment and tears in his eyes. Ava squeezed me so hard, I thought she would break my rib cage. Then of course we cried like little babies.

Soloman cleared his throat. We turned to face him. He straightened his tie. "I think you've got it from here. I'll...be in touch," he nodded stiffly.

187

I threw my arms around his neck, eliciting a grunt from him, causing him to stumble back a step in surprise. I looked back up at his chagrined expression, he was actually *blushing*. His tan skin was reddened at the cheeks. "I don't even know how to thank you *enough*. You saved my life, you're the *only* reason I'm *alive...*"

His teeth gleamed in a wide grin. "Think nothing of it, kid."

I hugged him one last time, then left with my dad and Ava. Ava wouldn't leave my side for a few days, setting up camp in my room like she was preparing for a prolonged sleepover. My dad didn't mind one bit. In fact, he welcomed her to stay as long as she'd like. I knew it was mostly because he had to work at the library during the day to fill in for me and didn't like leaving me alone. I felt like everyone was trying to be cautious around me, like they were waiting for me to have a breakdown. I finally forced Ava away after the third day and told her to go back to her husband.

A few weeks later, I returned to work and started back classes for the fall semester. Life was continuing as normal again, well normal enough. I still had the nightmares and they came frequently. I always woke drenched in sweat and screaming. I was relieved to live with my dad, unsure of how I'd *ever* feel comfortable enough to live on my own. I was all the more relieved when I got my period. I had been feeling unsure of how I'd handle the situation if I *had* gotten pregnant.

I was having dinner with my dad when I got the call. The ring seemed to reverberate through the walls. My stomach flipped and I felt nauseous when I saw the number. My dad saw my expression and stopped eating.

"Detective Jacobs," I croaked.

"*They got him*," he said.

CHAPTER TWENTY-SIX

The Letter

They had found him in Spain, traveling by boat. He *had* changed his appearance, the old woman in France had witnessed correctly. I was called in to identify him in a line up, before they could press any charges. I felt like running the other way as soon as I pulled up to the station. But my dad nodded to me in encouragement. "Do what you gotta do, sweetheart."

Detective Jacobs was there of course, to meet me at the door. But when I turned around, my dad was suddenly behind me. I glanced at him questionably. "I want to see the son of a bitch who did this to my daughter," he uttered.

Detective Jacobs only nodded in acknowledgment, then led the way to the heavy door. I paused and took a deep breath before I walked through the threshold of it as Soloman held it open for me. I walked slowly behind him, with my eyes trained to the ground. My pulse was doing that drumming thing in my ears again, the way it always did when *he* was near. My dad followed silently behind. I stopped when Soloman did, still not raising my eyes.

"Alright, Violet, when you're ready, take a good look. You don't have to speak. Just nod, okay?" he said in a soothing voice.

I raised my eyes and spotted him immediately, but he looked so *different*. He looked ridiculous with his dyed black, chopped hair. His skin was as tan as leather now, from hours in the open sun. He wore a smug expression on his face. But those same golden eyes stared back at me through the glass. It unnerved me. I felt like he was watching me and I started to panic. I gasped, turning around. *"Number three, it's number three,"* I blurted out before Soloman could even ask me. "Can I *leave now?*" I didn't even realize I was shaking.

With a quick nod to the officers inside of the window, Soloman answered. "Yes, Violet, you can leave now," he assured me. "You did great."

I started to walk back on my own, towards the door. My dad hung back a fraction longer, staring through the glass. I could tell he was committing Diego's face to memory. *"Dad.."* I called and he turned and followed, a begrudging look on his face.

After Diego was charged, the trial seemed to take forever. Luckily, he was being held with no bond, thanks to my attorney. Yet, every night I couldn't sleep. Six very long and stressful months later, the trial had finally came. By then I had recovered somewhat and felt much stronger than I had before. There was no way he was walking, with a murder charge and one attempted murder. But I had to testify, nonetheless, after Ava. Diego was barely allowed to speak, my defense attorney had badgered him into a corner so well. I didn't shake as I recalled our traumatic relationship, word for word, start to bloody finish.

"I hope you *rot* for what you did to me. And I'll happily get to watch you do just that. I'm sure *Trinity* would be happy, too." I spat my last words to him.

The jury decided in less than an hour. Guilty of all crimes, life in prison with no chance of parole. He was to be sent to Mexico, to go to trial there for his crimes. He would serve a life sentence here in the U.S., and a life sentence in Mexico if convicted, not that he'd ever get that far.

He didn't have any last words. As I watched him get taken away in handcuffs, I knew it was finally *really* over. Me, my dad and Ava embraced, grateful for it all to be done with.

Four years later......

I packed up for the day, collecting the homework assignments, and slipping them into my briefcase to be graded later. I had been teaching fourth grade for three months now and I loved every minute. My life had finally moved on. My dad had taken over the library for me full time. I had moved out and into my own apartment with my boyfriend, Chris. I gathered my lunchbox and prepared to leave, when I heard my name being called.

"Ms. Crenshaw"

I looked up. "Yes, Kathleen?"

The small woman walked over and handed me a note. "Sorry, I know you're about to leave. You have a letter."

Confused, I wondered why I had received it so late and why it hadn't been put in my mailbox like all of my other letters, but I took it anyway. "Oh, thank you Kathleen."

"No problem, are we still on for dinner this Friday?" she hovered by my desk, pushing back her short, sandy blonde hair.

"Yes, yes of course." We had always had a late teacher's luncheon on Friday's at whoever's turn it was to pick for the week's favorite restaurant.

She nodded. "Good, well have a good night."

"You too," I called after her a moment too late, as she retreated out of the door and into the hall.

My mind was too preoccupied by the ominous white envelope in my hands. I turned it over, but it had no writing on either side. I dashed the fear out of my mind. It was probably just late field trip money from one of the student's parents in my class. I tore it open, but found no money, nor a check. A single piece of paper was folded neatly. I opened it with shaking hands.

My little dove, I've found you.

I dropped the note and watched it slide to my feet. I felt frozen where I stood. I wanted to scream, but I was paralyzed. My pulse began to drum in my ears again. My palms, back, neck and forehead were clammy. My eyes scanned the hallway and windows furiously, terrified to find a dark figure lurking close by.

My phone rang in the empty classroom, the shrill sound echoing through the walls. My back arched and chills ran down my arms. It took me a minute to force my feet to move, but I finally did. The cement legs that were my own, took two steps towards my purse on the desk. I reached into it and pulled out my phone, eyeing the screen cautiously. It was detective Jacobs.

"Hel— hello?"

"*Violet, where are you?*" he sounded winded, like he was walking quickly.

"I'm...I'm at work," I answered slowly.

"*Stay there, I'm coming to get you,*" he commanded.

"*Why?*" I whispered, already on the verge of tears. But what Soloman didn't know was, I wasn't asking why he was coming, because I *knew*. I was asking why.. *why* was this happening. I had *finally* picked up the pieces of my shattered life. I'd glued myself back together like a broken porcelain doll. I had finally begun to heal and move on. *Why now?*

"*Diego has escaped,*" Soloman said.

To Be Continued...

CHAPTER TWENTY-SEVEN
He Loves Me Not

Stay tuned for the sequel to He Loves Me...

He Loves Me Not

Coming August 2020

Made in the USA
Coppell, TX
03 August 2020